WAITING ON CHRISTMAS

WAITING

ON

CHRISTMAS

A Holiday Romance Novel

KATIE BACHAND

MINNEAPOLIS, MN

ISBN **978-1-7334326-8-9**

FIRST EDITION

Cover Illustration and Design by Lance Buckley Design
Book Design by KB
Author Image by Studio Twelve:52

Waiting on Christmas is a fiction novel. Names, characters, places, incidents and plot lines are used fictitiously and are a result of the author's imagination. Thus meaning, any resemblance to persons alive or deceased, buildings, establishments, locals, or events is coincidental.

For Grandma Dolly.

As we celebrate our first Christmas apart,

I'll always hold you in my heart.

BOOKS BY KATIE BACHAND

(click the book title you're interested to navigate to the Amazon sales page!)

SERIES
Becoming Us (Prequel)
Conflict of Interest (#1)
In the Business of Love (#2)
A Business Affair (#3)
Betting on Us (#4)

STANDALONE
The Problem with Love Potions

HOLIDAY
Postmark Christmas
Waiting on Christmas
A Borrowed Christmas Love Story
The Worst Christmas Wife

JOIN KATIE'S NEWSLETTER!

Head to Katie's website at
www.katiebachandauthor.com
and join her newsletter for fun content, great
deals, free books, and more.

Or, simply scan the QR code below.
(Reading a physical copy? Hover your phone camera over the image!)

Enjoy!

WAITING ON CHRISTMAS

PROLOGUE

Finley Whittaker had been up since six that morning. It was tough to get up that early since she'd stayed up late weighing her options. And that was after she'd celebrated Thanksgiving late into the night with family and friends at the farm. But, as a ten-year-old – almost eleven – she could handle it.

Today was Day One of her mission.

Day One, because what she had to find out couldn't be done in a single day. It would take time, careful planning, a lot of spying, and really good investigative work.

This season, she would find out if Santa Claus was real. And what better place to find the truth than their own Christmas tree farm?

Winter Haven Tree Farm, Finley imagined, was a lot like the North Pole. Everybody that worked there was a Christmas fanatic. They had shops, food, around-the-clock hot chocolate, horse and sleigh rides, and of course, Santa Claus.

Finley tied her hair in a long black braid that hung over her shoulder, slid tall brown work boots over her jeans, and hopped off the bed. She analyzed the farm schedule her mom had printed off the night before – it might have been Thanksgiving, but Fran Whittaker didn't leave any detail untouched, unplanned, or unscheduled.

Moving her finger down the hours of the day, Finley stopped when she saw *Santa Claus, pictures and presents.*

Three PM, Finley noted, and nodded to herself. Just enough time to finish chores, help with the bakery, eat lunch with Maeve, then start her mission.

"Lee, you ready?"

She heard her dad's voice echo up the stairs and into her room and grinned. She liked the nickname her dad used for her; it made her feel tough, cool, older.

"Lee?"

"Coming!" She didn't want to make her dad wait. He was a hard worker and she liked showing she could work just as hard as he could.

Turning back only once to snatch the schedule, she quickly folded it, shoved the uneven edges of it into her pocket, and rushed out of her bedroom door.

Her boots sounded like a stampede as she raced down the stairs. She skidded down the last three with the heels of her boots barely making contact with the wooden steps. As she slid, she grabbed her thick work jacket off its hook then landed firmly at the base. Without thinking she slid her arms into the jacket, pulled her hat out of one pocket and reached for her gloves in the other.

At the creak in the floor, she looked up and grinned as her dad joined her in the entryway. When she saw the gift box her dad was holding behind his back, she couldn't help the enthusiastic smile that splayed across her face.

"One early Christmas present for my girl. Don't tell your mom." Charlie Whittaker winked at his daughter and pulled the present out from behind his back.

Shreds of wrapping paper flew from the package and landed on the floor as her hands moved efficiently around the box, opening it like she did every year when her dad walked in with one early gift. This time though, as she studied the contents, she didn't know how to feel.

In a way, looking at what lay in front of her, she felt older, wiser. In another it felt as though it was a sign she *needed* to grow up. But, most of all, it's what she'd always wanted. It wasn't a new stuffed animal, barrette, or colorful earrings.

Finley reached in and grabbed the thick, rust-colored leather work gloves – the ones that looked just like her dad's – and looked up with pride.

"What do you think, kiddo?"

Finley nodded her agreement at first, her words lost, but finally looked up and said, "This is the best early Christmas present I've ever gotten. Thanks, dad."

She slid the gloves on and curled her fingers in them a couple times, then launched toward her dad to wrap in him in a hug. Maybe because she was ten she shouldn't hug her dad like this anymore, but they were inside where no one could see, and she did just get the coolest present. When she felt her dad give her a big squeeze then plant a kiss on the top of her stocking cap, she let go and grinned.

"Ready, Lee?" her dad asked.

Finley stood tall with her arms at her side and said, "Ready."

Then she walked out the door with her dad, the chill of winter greeting her with a cool gust of wind, ready for her tenth holiday season at the farm.

They usually started in the hills and worked their way down. Finley grinned when Old Bobby Mills told her an entire row of cutting was her responsibility and to just, 'load 'em on up into the back of the truck when she was done.'

Finley liked Old Bobby, but she didn't really think he seemed all that old. She understood it was a nickname but thought it should at least make a little bit of sense. Shrugging off the idea she watched her dad and Bobby walk down a row or two of trees, pointing and nodding, forming their plan. They'd cut some trees today, haul them down to Haven's base, and sell them to the people that didn't want to venture up and cut their own tree down.

Grabbing her saw, she carried it to the first tree in the line that was now officially her duty, and started sawing away at the base.

3

She'd learned years ago how to saw, how to keep your movements fluid, where to cut, and how to make the tree fall in the direction you wanted it to go.

After three cuts, three trees laid out neatly in a row. Finley smiled to herself and sat back on her heels to take a small break and guzzle some of the water her dad had packed for them. From where she was sitting, Finley could see all of Haven's base – what they called the main attraction area where the offices, shops, and bakery were – and already saw movement. It was early, but it didn't stop the rush or the excitement on a day like today.

The day after Thanksgiving was like living in a new world. It's like time flipped a switch and suddenly everything was magical. Christmas music sang from speakers mounted to tall wooden poles, the scent of cinnamon, molasses, and peppermint took the place of savory rosemary and sweet pumpkin, and twinkle lights were strung, wrapped, and circled around every building, post, and tree.

Then there was that. Finley let out a small giggle to herself as she heard laughter coming from one of the sleigh rides that started at seven-thirty sharp. She was a kid herself, but there was something contagious about the way it sounded to her. It was her favorite sound. She heard it nonstop around Christmastime, and especially when Santa Claus made his appearance.

The idea of seeing Santa today, for the first time in a year – which seemed like an eternity – had her picking up the saw once more to finish the job she was tasked to do. Maybe if she hurried she'd get time off after lunch to prepare for Santa. Do a little pre-mission recon. Maybe Maeve would be able to help her once the lunch crowd died down a bit.

Yes, that's exactly what she would do, she thought, as the next tree tipped to the ground next to the others.

"What do you have left to do?" Maeve asked as she dipped the corner of a grilled cheese sandwich into a bowl full of homemade tomato soup.

"Nothing. I finished everything. This isn't something to take lightly, you know. Will you be able to come with me?"

"Dunno," Maeve answered through a bite then paused to finish before going on. "Mom said she could use my help with the afternoon cookies. I'll let you know. Come back and check if I'm done before you go spy. I want to see every move Santa makes."

Finley appreciated the determination in Maeve's eyes. Maeve was her best friend, so she was pretty sure Maeve would have been up for whatever kind of mission Finley set out on, but she was also a firm believer in Santa Claus. Maeve would need every possible piece of proof Santa wasn't real before she could be told otherwise. Which, Finley thought, was exactly why she wouldn't want to miss out on spying. The only thing that would keep Maeve from joining, was cookies.

"Okay, I'll be back. I want to run over to the shop."

"I saw Stacy and Clara." Maeve's dreamy look let Finley know she was imagining an older version of herself. "They're the ones working today. You should see how cool they look. You can tell they're in high school now. I can't wait to be in high school. I want to be just like them."

"Yeah, I saw their names on the schedule, that's why I'm going. Last week, when they were setting up, Clara let me use her mascara and lip gloss. I'm saving to get my own."

"I'm jealous. Mom told me no makeup until I'm thirteen. That's so far away."

Finley didn't want to say she wasn't allowed to wear makeup either, but she'd already decided that's what she was going to spend her saved-up money on, so even if she couldn't wear it with her parents around, she'd still have it.

"Maeve, are you about finished up?" Marvel Robb, Maeve's mom, snuck her plump head around the corner of the kitchen to get a look at the girls.

Maeve slouched at the call, but only for show, because really, she liked making cookies. The idea of mixing and sampling dough all afternoon sounded really great.

"Finished! Coming," Maeve called out without turning. "See you later?"

"Definitely."

"Okay, don't forget to stop by before you start spying."

"Deal."

The day was already going better than expected. Stacy and Clara, who were officially the coolest. Both girls went in on a Christmas present for Finley, and gave it to her when she stopped by. Her own mini-makeup set. When she opened the shimmering powders and sparkling lip glosses she knew she didn't play it cool, but she was too excited to hide her wide smile and the shock of feeling so grown up.

She also knew she spent way too much time in the shop and had to go set up for her mission. Finley longed to try her new makeup, but all she had time for was a quick swipe of the pink gloss before she carefully stowed it in the top drawer of her dresser and dashing out again.

"Maeve, you back there?" Finley yelled over the bakery counter through thick puffs of breath.

"Yeah. Cookies. Gingerbread. I can't make it."

Finley grinned at the quick clip of words, knowing Maeve would have stayed for any cookie, and that was okay. She could do her recon on her own. She'd report back with all of the details Maeve would require the next time they saw each other.

"Okay, see you later?"

"Yeah. But Lee," Maeve's voice was urgent, "remember, I want to know *everything.*"

"You got it. Bye."

Finley didn't waste a second and ran toward Santa's workshop. Inside, Santa had a big wooden chair, woodsy garland, lights, and flocks of snow all around him. She didn't understand why Santa needed a chair that size, but she supposed it was pretty cool and it made sense that somebody as great as Santa would get to sit in it. Her Grandma said it was carved by hand using the very trees they had on their farm. That was cool too, she decided.

Inching her way around to the back door of the shop, Finley climbed two bales of hay that sat just below one of the workshop windows. It gave her the perfect spot to watch Santa as he walked in and got ready. If it was like all the times before, he'd walk in wearing a big brown jacket lined with fur, nothing that normal people really wore, and big black boots with matching black gloves. He even kind of looked like Santa when he wasn't dressed all in red. Then he would go to the back room, change into his berry-colored suit and matching hat, then come out holding his belly, laughing as if wearing the suit was the happiest thing he'd ever done.

Lost in her daydream, Finley nearly missed Santa's arrival. When he walked into the room she hurried to duck so she wouldn't be caught spying, but as she lowered herself her hand slipped off the bale and she toppled to the ground with a little squeal.

"Hey, are you okay?"

Flat on her back, Finley tried to catch the breath the hard ground slapped out of her, then looked around for the voice. When the face appeared, she figured the boy couldn't have been much older than she was. He stood over her showing off a crooked grin. Then he said again, "You okay?"

"Y.eah. I think I got out of the way in time, too," Finley answered, not worried about injuries, and more concerned that her mission had been compromised.

"Got out of the way?" the boy questioned, and held out a hand.

Finley took the offered hand, stood, and wiped the dirt off the back of her jeans.

"Yeah, I'm on a mission."

"Nice. What kind?" he asked, intrigued.

Eyeing the boy, she tried to judge just how much she could trust him. And more importantly, if he would think she was silly for the mission she was on in the first place. Cocking her head to the right, she eyed the boy, and decided he was worthy.

"It's a Santa Claus mission." Finley waited to see what kind of reaction she would get. When there was only a nod of understanding she continued. "I have a lot of friends at school that told me Santa isn't real. But I see him close up every year and don't really have a reason to believe he isn't. I mean, he makes all the kids that see him here really happy. So, I'm spying on Santa this year to find out for myself. If he's not real, I'll see it. I'll know."

The boy only nodded again, taking in what he'd heard.

"My brother told me Santa was fake. That only babies believed in him. Well, just my older brother, Jake. James, my younger brother is like me. We're believers."

It was Finley's turn to nod.

"I'm Lee." She held out her hand. "If you want to, you can join my mission. I think it would be nice to know. And my friend Maeve couldn't come so I don't have anybody to spy with."

The boy took her hand and said, "I'm Jackson, and I'm in."

The night had gotten cold by the time Finley came in from her second round of spying, stopping only once because her mom had made her come in for dinner. Now, she was shivering, and exhausted. After a quick shower she went down for a cookie and to kiss her parent's good night, before climbing the stairs and eventually into bed. The big clock on the wall leading up the stairs had told her it was just after eleven, and she had to be ready for another day of chores around sunrise.

But, even with her eyes heavy and wilting, she smiled at the day. She and Jackson had watched Santa Claus call kids by their names, give deep, rolling laughs as kids looked on in amazement that he already knew what they wanted for Christmas. During the mission they sipped hot chocolate and snacked on cookies while they watched Santa sneak to the back room to steal bites of his own stash of cookies when nobody was watching.

After two hours they had both agreed: Santa Claus wasn't only real, he must use magic almost all the time.

Jackson had to go back to his family for a while to take pictures with Santa and to pick out a tree. But they ended up staying for the first movie of the season – *Miracle on 34th Street*, a family favorite – so before it started he was able to sneak away and found Finley wandering the tree lot. They watched two people hold hands, and when Jackson held hers – thinking that's what you were supposed to do while looking for trees – Finley let him. It was a little surprising, but she thought it felt nice.

They walked and talked for as long as they could. Jackson asked Finley what it was like to live on the farm and get to do cool things like cut down trees and eat cookies all day. She didn't want to make him feel badly but she admitted it was the best thing in the whole world.

When the movie had just about come to an end Finley couldn't help but feel sad that Jackson had to leave. She tried to be as cool as she could when she walked next to him toward the parking lot where his family was waiting, but she felt as though her heart was tightening inside her body.

Even now, lying in bed, she kind of missed him. But, she lifted her hand to her cheek as her eyelids fell towards a night full of dreams, he had promised that he would be back the same time next year, then kissed her cheek before turning and running the final stretch to his family.

...

One year later, one year older and wiser, Finley found herself in bed after a long day once again. Only this time, her heart was a little less full. She brought her hand to her cheek as she had many nights over the past year, anticipating this very day. Now the day had come and gone. She couldn't remember any particular detail of it since she'd spent most of it trying to find Jackson in the crowds that wandered in and out. She'd sat until the very end of the movie, not really watching, just waiting.

When the last family had huddled into their van with a tree strapped tightly to its roof, she stood alone under the lamppost and watched it drive away.

Finley sucked in a breath as she had when the snow had begun to drift down around her, holding back the small trickle of emotion that tried to escape. She didn't want to believe Jackson didn't come, but the fact was that he hadn't been there. But she was too old to feel sad about it for too long. So, rather than get upset, Finley had wiped her leather glove across her nose, sniffed, and swore that whenever Jackson could make it back, she would be there to see him.

Closing her eyes, Finley let herself drift into an exhausted sleep, with just a bit of hope that she'd see Jackson again one winter day.

Waiting on Christmas

CHAPTER 1

Finley stared out of the farmhouse kitchen toward the rustic buildings that would be bustling with activity come morning. They didn't often get snow as early as Thanksgiving, but this year it added to her view.

A lot had changed over the years, she thought as she looked out. They'd expanded, added pretty little log cabins along the edge of the woods for people to rent, updated their structures, bought more land higher into the hills for growing the evergreen trees that would decorate the homes of families near and far. But, as she took in Santa's workshop at the end of a long line of buildings, she remembered the day, twenty years ago, when a young boy had stolen her heart and never returned to give it back.

How often had she wondered about him and where he'd gone? Possibly every day since.

"I would offer you something stronger than your dad's Apple Pie, but I feel like it still wouldn't do."

Finley angled her head and grinned as Maeve walked up beside her and draped an arm over her shoulder. When their heads came together Finley sighed, not quite knowing what had her feeling so exhausted. Was it the workload? The start of another season? Or was it never quite letting go of Jackson?

The last thought had a pitiful, breathy laugh escaping with it. Why in the world was she even still thinking about him? It was *one* day, twenty years ago. So maybe her exhaustion was due to how pathetic she was being.

"Are you going to tell me what it is? Or are you going to make me guess?" Maeve asked, breaking contact to turn and lean on the counter. "I am a good guesser but I have an early morning. I'm not sure if you know, but tomorrow's a pretty big day around here."

Finley mimicked Maeve's move and leaned her own hip against the brown granite. She folded her arms and let the tumbler of Apple Pie rest in one hand on top.

Another deep breath escaped, she shook her head and looked up.

"I don't even know. I feel tired and the season hasn't even started. There's so much to do, day in and day out. I guess I'm just wondering, well," Finley paused, feeling ashamed of the thought, much less that she was about to say it out loud, "is this all worth it? Is it *really* what I want to do with the rest of my life?"

Finley watched the small, caring smile settle on Maeve's face, and the tilt of her head that offered understanding.

"You've been running the farm for five years now. You could do it in your sleep." Maeve eyed Finley, dipping her head slightly to regain their gaze. "But doing it in your sleep is different than loving it."

Remaining quiet, because she didn't know what else to say, Finley took a sip from her glass and turned to look outside.

Did she not love it anymore? Was that *really* it? The reason she was feeling so anxious, yet so tired?

She could do this job in her sleep. The movements, the rhythm, the people, all of it so familiar. Like a habit or daily ritual. She was on autopilot.

"Lee," Maeve began, breaking into Finley's thoughts, "why don't you use the rest of this year, this season, and try and *enjoy it*? Really take the time to appreciate everything. Slow down enough to smell the pine in the air; the cinnamon and sweet spice from the bakery. Take a sleigh ride rather than give one. Walk through the tree lot with the best cup of hot chocolate – because you *know* we have the best."

Finley grinned at the comment. Of course, they had the best. Maeve had taken the bakery over from her mother when she returned from culinary school, along with all food operations. That meant they had the most talented baker, making the world's best hot chocolate, right there at their small-town, Minnesota tree farm.

Finley still got a chuckle out of Maeve's parents requiring an education, even though they knew – as well as everybody else that knew Maeve – she'd be right back at the farm doing what she loved the most.

Giving in just a bit, but mostly to help with her argument, Finley agreed, "We do have the best hot chocolate."

"There's my girl."

"But…"

"Ah, there she is again." Maeve smirked.

"Ha-ha, very funny. *But,* there's too much to do, to keep in order, to just drift through my day."

"I'm not sure if you noticed, but you have an obsessively organized, slightly over-eager, bordering-on-neurotic cousin, who's carrying on your mother's detail-oriented bloodline. You couldn't get off track if you left for the whole month of December. I'm not saying we all wouldn't be miserable," Maeve said while imagining the twenty-something becoming their new lieutenant, then shaking it off like she'd just gotten a glimpse of a horror film, "but if Blair had to run the show for a bit, we'd survive."

"I don't know."

"And, it would give you more time to be on the lookout for Jackson." Maeve covered her heart and gave an exaggerated, wistful look. "The ten-year-old that got away."

"That is *not* what I do."

Maeve shifted her eyes and let the little roll speak for her.

"That's not what I do all the time."

Finley sighed and sipped. She supposed it wouldn't be the worst thing in the world if she didn't work herself to the bone. She could take some time to slow down, or at least pause and *try* and appreciate little moments throughout her day. After all, she used to love it – everything about it.

"I can see by your blank stare you're starting to agree with me, so I'm going to add a little nudge. Don't spend the season waiting on Christmas this year. Enjoy the whole season for everything it has to offer. Then, after you've *really* tried, you'll know for sure if this is something you want to do for the rest of your life. And just keep on doing that, year after year. Maybe you'll decide it's not what you want, but you'll have given it a shot. Or, maybe," Maeve said, shrugging and clinking her glass to Finley's, "maybe you'll realize you still love it."

The women stood shoulder to shoulder enjoying a couple minutes of uninterrupted thought and drinking time. But they nearly spit up their last sip when the whole family piled in at once, all of them laughing, chattering, and a few arguing over football.

"There you are!" Fran Whittaker burst through the swinging kitchen door with her glass and a new jar of Apple Pie held high. "We wondered where you two snuck off to. We have celebrating to do. Christmas season might be starting, and it might be late, but it's still Thanksgiving and I'm going to get every ounce of party out of the day I can before we head south."

Fran and her husband, Charlie, had been migrating to the South Carolina coastline since their daughter had taken the reins. They squawked and squabbled about missing family and the snow, but that didn't stop them from sending hordes of pictures of themselves sharing bonfires with new friends, walks along the beach, and warm and sunny days spent lounging.

Finley knew they loved it, and she had to admit, it gave her a certain peace of mind knowing they were enjoying themselves after years of hard work. She didn't think warm winters were for her, but maybe someday she'd settle down, and slow down, enough to enjoy a lazy season.

Though, it would be nice to have somebody to be lazy with.

The thought flashed into her mind with the image of a young Jackson. Then she admonished herself for even having the thought. But how many times had she imagined what he looked like now? Wondered what he was doing, where he was working? Or, if he ever thought about her?

Silly. That's just silly.

"I'll drink to that!" Miles Booker, Maeve's husband, joined in on the celebration by taking the jar, twisting off the lid, then making his way around the room, refilling any glass shallower than half full.

Finley watched hers fill to the brim and shot Maeve an eye. When Maeve simply shrugged and held out her own glass, Finley knew she was out numbered. Though, it didn't stop her grin as Blair maneuvered to her side to hold up her own glass. She was twenty-one, but just. Finley gave her elbow a little nudge and earned a smile. At least if she was going to be weary from a night of celebrating, she wouldn't be the only one.

Then she saw the enormous three-ring binder hanging at Blair's side.

Well, she thought, celebrating *and* working. They'd be weary, but organized.

The night turned into one filled with card games, *A Charlie Brown Thanksgiving,* more drinks, and when everybody wandered back into the kitchen they couldn't believe they were about to have a second dose of Thanksgiving dinner – though they'd sworn off eating only hours earlier.

By the time the food was repacked, everything had quieted. Many had left for home or toward the new little cabins they were staying in for the night. Maeve and Miles had made their way home too. They'd have the earliest day of them all, prepping the bakery, then meals for the masses that would crowd the farm.

Finley said goodnight to her parents who slowly crept up the stairs to their longtime bedroom, then glanced outside once more. It was late, but she wanted to clear her mind before making her own way up. Piling on her winter coat, her work boots, and the third pair of leather gloves she'd gone through over the years, she made her way out into the lightly falling snow.

It was barely covering the ground, and tomorrow it might well be melted away as the ground wasn't quite cold enough to hold the frozen flakes, but tonight it looked beautiful. The farm was lit by large floodlights on huge wooden poles, looking like beacons throughout the base and into the pine trees on the hill. Twinkle lights were now strung and would be showing off their sparkle around the clock until the new year. And along the gravel paths, lanterns with big red bows guided the way to the shops.

Now, they led her to a spot she'd been coming to for twenty years. At first she went there hoping, waiting. As time went on, the hay bales sitting beneath the window outside of Santa's shop became a place for her to sit and think.

Today, as she sat, she decided she'd take Maeve's advice. She would slow down enough to enjoy the season. Take in the beauty – because it was beautiful.

Finley breathed deeply and closed her eyes, letting the cool speckles of snow land softly on her face.

'Stop waiting on Christmas.'

Maeve's words replayed in her mind, and she nodded to nobody in particular. She wouldn't let the days simply slip by her this year. She wouldn't wake up to realize Christmas had come and gone. She'd take the time, take in the small moments, enjoy the beauty, and Lord knew she'd enjoy the food. Then, and really only then, would she sit down at the end of the season and make a decision about her future at the farm. And if that decision happened to be that she no longer be a part of it, she'll know she'd given it time, and enjoyed what might be her last.

CHAPTER 2

There wouldn't be daylight for another three hours. Four in the morning was early, but over the years, Finley had trained herself to throw the covers off, walk across the room to turn off her alarm clock, slide her slippers on, and walk down the stairs to brew the first roasty pot of coffee. She didn't think about the movements; if she did she probably would have rolled over and savored the warmth of the blankets protecting her from the cold.

Turning the corner into the kitchen, Finley screamed as she was met with an enthusiastic greeting.

"Good morning! Happy first day of Christmas!"

Finley clutched her chest as she watched Blair dart from one side of the kitchen to the other, pulling orange juice and muffins out of the fridge, then back to the coffee pot to pour a second steaming mug.

Enjoy it.

The thought seemed more like a mantra than a reminder as she forced her breathing and her heart to slow. But as quickly as the mantra came, it was replaced with action. Finley smiled and took the offered mug from the young woman whose smile stretched the length of her face. And in slowing down just a bit, she noticed Blair donned skinny jeans, a flannel shirt, and a single long braid that dangled over her shoulder.

"Thanks," Finley said, keeping her grin to herself and savoring the first hot sip.

She wondered if she would have even taken the time to notice, and to appreciate, that Blair was dressed exactly as Finley would be for the workday ahead.

"Okay." Blair looked up from the seat she'd taken in the breakfast nook, wondering if Finley was going to join her. Satisfied when Finley started to move, she continued. "I have the schedule ready for the week. Let's start with today; from the top and work our way down."

Nodding as an agenda was placed in front of her, Finley took another sip and read while Blair talked her through it, just as she did with her parents when it was her turn to take over. She remembered the pride in her parents' eyes and the satisfied feeling of knowing she'd put it there.

"Bobby is starting early this morning to bring down the first load of trees. He's going to make cuts and rounds through noon and assess the inventory. Grandpa Chuck is working the tree stand this year with Blake. Blake knows to do most of the heavy lifting." Blair smiled sweetly as they both knew their Grandpa would try and work as if he was the same age as her younger brother: eighteen with energy and stamina that could compete with the Clydesdales they had tromping around giving sleigh rides.

"We'll never get rid of him," Finley joked lovingly about the eighty-three-year-old man.

"Never. But Blake does have basketball practice and a couple of games coming up, we'll need some help. Bobby said he'll pitch in, but you and I might be in the game."

"That's no problem." Finley liked the idea of working with her Grandpa, remembering her promise to enjoy the season, that seemed like a good place to start. "Okay, what else?"

"Maeve and Miles pulled in when I woke up. I ran out to say 'good morning,' offered them the last open cabin again. They still turned it down."

"I suppose we'll let them enjoy their new stunning farmhouse on the edge of town."

"Yeah, I guess. I miss them being here though."

"Me too."

Over the next thirty minutes they walked through gift shop details, Santa's schedule, wreath-making, and the double-feature of *Miracle on 34th Street* that would start at six – sharp. Only a couple times while Blair was talking did Finley's mind drift to her cousin, letting the tasks flutter in and out, having heard them all before it wasn't hard.

Young and energetic, not unlike Blair's younger brother, were the words that came to mind. They were hard workers. Tedious even. When she'd let Blair take on the schedule only a year before she remembered feeling annoyed, bothered at the constant ordering and organization. But now, as she looked on and felt the hint of guilt wash over her, she realized she'd missed the young woman's intentions. Rather than show pride or thanks, Finley had been dismissive. Rather than see she was being imitated, it irked her. That had been wrong, and Finley knew it. Blair deserved a chance – then and now.

As if on cue, Blair straightened her back and shoulders and looked Finley in the eye.

"There's one more thing I'd like to talk to you about."

"Okay, ready when you are."

"I know last year you felt it was too much work, or maybe you didn't feel I was ready."

Blair's introduction left a sting and an appropriate amount of shame. Finley had brushed Blair off at a request she was sure was about to come again.

"But, I'd like you to consider me taking on another project at the farm. I want the responsibility, I'm ready for it. You wouldn't have to do anything, or not right away. I think we should expand."

Blair paused and held her breath, waiting for dismissal. When none came, she exhaled and continued.

"I'll go through the list of proposals we got last year and ones we've gotten this year from vendors and retailers looking to partner with us. I'll put together the best ones and bring them to you. If after I present them, if you don't feel like it's the right move, that's okay, but, well, maybe you will."

The tenacity didn't surprise her. Neither did the confidence to ask again. Blair was ambitious. The part that did though, was how Finley felt. Not about Blair, but about her own ambition. When had she become a *settler?*

Looking at Blair – actually looking, and listening – she realized in her own struggles, and getting lost in the busy work of the farm and the season, she'd missed opportunities. She'd held people – her friends and family – back. She'd settled and forced others to do the same.

"How about this. As you find the time, put together what you want to talk to me about. You don't need to wait until the end of the season. We'll make time when you're ready."

"Really?" Excitement electrified the room until Blair used every ounce of willpower to act professionally. "I mean, yes, yes, I'll do that. Thank you, Lee."

"Of course. Well," Finley said, as she pushed away from the table, "I better get dressed. We have a big season ahead of us."

As Finley stood Blair did the same, but before she could walk back out of the kitchen Blair leapt toward her cousin and wrapped her arms around her. She squeezed so tightly Finley had to let out a small laugh and give a little squeeze in return.

"Thank you." The whisper was so small, but overflowing with appreciation.

Finley placed a kiss on the top of the dark, braided hair, squeezed once more, then let go, winking on her way out.

Not a bad way to start. She felt genuinely happy as she dressed herself in the same uniform she had for years, now looking like Blair's twin. Her long hair had more of a wave to it and wisps seemed to fall throughout the day, driving her crazy until she'd shove it in a stocking cap, but everything else – from the straight body that wore the same skinny jeans to the flannel shirt – hit the mark.

Not ten minutes later when she skipped down the stairs, she saw the thermos of coffee waiting by her boots.

"Nice touch, Blair." Finley pulled her boots on then grabbed her second dose of caffeine. Yes, it was definitely going to be a good day.

CHAPTER 3

"Get your head out of the woods, Jack. It's time to grow up. We aren't going to make it on happy thoughts and Christmas miracles. Santa Claus doesn't tend to stick his nose into business. We actually have to work for what we want. And what we want – and need – is something concrete. Something that involves the community. And, I can't believe I'm saying this, that shows we believe in the Christmas spirit as much as the little mom-and-pop shop down the road. But," there was *always* a 'but,' "it still needs to be profitable."

Obviously, his blank stare and silence didn't satisfy his older brother. Jackson watched Jake run his hands through his hair, a sure sign of exasperation and frustration. But what was he supposed to do about it? He thought his idea of a charitable donation of a part of their profits was a great idea – and a tax write off. Apparently, and as his father kindly, if slightly disappointingly reminded him, 'that also eliminates a part of their profits.'

Well, he guessed it was a point worth taking, but it still wasn't a bad idea.

Jackson shifted in his seat, playing with the uncomfortable tie he'd worn for their meeting today. They might be family, but they also had an image to uphold, a company to run. And though he'd never tell his dad and brothers, he would happily trade in his suit and tie to work the ground floor of their retail stores, interact with their customers, and hear the stories of the adventures they'd have using their outdoor and recreational equipment. Or heck, take it one further, just quit all together, buy a few things, and haul the old tent out of storage that had sat too long without being used.

It seemed funny to him, they were a company that encouraged people to enjoy the outdoors, take in wildlife, appreciate nature. Yet here they were, crisp and slick sitting in a modern brick building, strategizing from the top floor.

"Jackson?" John Bloom, his own father, questioned tiredly, "are you with us?"

"Yes. I brought a great idea to the table." Jackson tried his best to recover since he had in fact been daydreaming. "Obviously it's not the direction we want to go in. I'll go back to the drawing board."

John only nodded his consent. "Why don't the three of you sit down?"

Since Jackson and his younger brother, James, were already sitting, they exchanged questioning looks first. Then everybody looked to Jake who gave a quick, barely noticeable shake of his head and started moving toward an open chair.

When his boys were sitting, John began, "I've been thinking about this a lot lately. Your mother and I have been talking. We think it's time I take retirement seriously. I've been putting it off due to our declining profits, but there's never going to be a perfect time. There will always be *something*."

The three men stared at their father and couldn't believe what they were hearing. Each having their own reason for disbelief, but all could agree that the man they were looking at now looked conflicted, and that wasn't one of the characteristics of the usually confident man.

"I'd really – no – it would be nice, to be able to retire knowing the three of you were getting along. That you were all in agreement with the direction of the company. Maybe you could work on that. I won't make any announcements until the new year but I think regardless, that's when I'll ride off into the proverbial sunset."

John gave a little laugh and continued. "That's what your mom tells me retirement is like: never-ending days of sunrises and sunsets – and whatever else you want to do in between."

It had been rare seeing his three sons share a laugh at the same time, but seeing it now at the loving expense of their ever-joyful mother, had John longing to see it a lot more.

He hoped they'd be able to work things out between the three of them. He'd learned the hard way working closely with family could be challenging. Luckily, he and his own brother had fought their way through the rocky parts and made it to the other side with only minor bumps and bruises.

Jackson knew getting up to take a 'breather' wasn't at all what his brothers had in mind when their father had left the room expecting them to start brainstorming, but he had to get out. It was stifling in there. And with his dad's announcement he was even more conflicted than before.

What did they really expect from him? A cure-all idea that would at the flip of a switch turn their profits black and all of their worries behind them? That didn't exist.

The idea guy, they used to call him. *Jack of all trades.*

At one point maybe he could have come up with that idea, that once-in-a-lifetime course of action that would help. That was when he was invested, hungry, fresh out of college and ready to take on the world. But now, he'd never felt so removed.

The fresh winter air would be a welcome change from the stuffy office. He didn't know where he was going when he started to walk out, but found himself pulling on his wool coat and turning for the elevator.

Overnight, he noticed, their office had become nature's version of decorating for the holidays. Christmas trees had been hauled in but didn't hold the ordinary shiny bulbs or ornaments. Instead they held small woodland creatures, garland of berries and nuts, clumpy flocks of snow, and the prop gifts that sat below were old wooden skis, and toboggans filled with stuffed animals in the shape of every wild creature you could imagine.

It was, he thought, perfect for their company and joyful enough to have him deciding on a quick walk to the coffee shop down the road to refuel. After all, it could be an extremely long day once he got back to the office.

Christmas music accompanied him and the rest of the city's residents, all who seemed to think getting coffee at nine that morning was a good idea.

"The day after Thanksgiving shoppers, I presume." The old man winked at Jackson and smiled. "I like to order ahead but it doesn't keep me from enjoying the crowd. I love a good crowd. I take mine straight black, then I add about a cup of sugar and as much cream as I can before somebody at the coffee station over there gives me the eye. How about you?"

Jackson couldn't help but stare. This poor old man must get so much grief this time of year. He looked like Santa Claus' twin. Right down to the white hair and rosy cheeks. He seemed jolly enough though, so maybe he wouldn't mind the attention.

"I take mine the same, hold the cream and sugar."

The old man howled out a laugh and touched a finger to his nose.

"Nick!" The barista shouted over the music and the crowd. "Two black coffees."

"Well look at that. It's your lucky day. Come on, it must be my day to treat."

Cautious, but eyeing the line, Jackson asked, "You're sure? You don't have anybody else who might like it more?"

"Not another in the world who might want it. The Missus is up north and I'm flying solo. C'mon."

Jackson nodded and offered a smile. "Then how can I turn it down?"

"Don't see why you'd wait until Christmas for a bit of magic and good luck. Say, what are you doing today? You look like a man that could use a break."

The smell coming from the warm cup reminded him of waking early and walking in snow-covered woods with a warm brew in hand. He took a scalding sip wondering if he should be concerned. Though he didn't know what to be more concerned about: that the old man might have actually used magic to conjure up two black coffees, or that his answer to the question asked of him wasn't 'no.'

"I thought I had a plan for the day, but I'm finding myself free at the moment." His brothers were going to kill him.

"Ah yes, those days are some of the best days. You look like a city slicker, but if I wasn't mistaken I bet I could take you for the outdoorsmen type."

"Got me again."

The two men navigated through the line of people waiting for their order and fell into step side-by-side when they made it outside to the sidewalk.

"Say, I'm not sure if this is something you'd be interested in, but I'm heading somewhere where I think they could use my help. If I'm right, they could use a bit of an outdoorsman. What do you say, want to help out an old man today? Put in some good old-fashioned hard work?"

The idea of ditching the office for a day outside sounded so good to him he nearly shouted his agreement. But there was the fact that it was a complete stranger asking him to tag along with him to a place yet to be named.

Jackson analyzed the offer and the man. The offer could have been just about anything and he would have taken it. The man? Well, if he was crazy, Jackson liked his odds of winning a foot-race to escape.

He went with something that showed interest but allowed for him to back out easily. "Sounds intriguing. Where are you headed today?"

"Lovely little place, though I guess I can hardly call it little anymore. They've grown quite a bit since I've been there last. A tree farm, Winter Haven Tree Farm."

Jackson came to a dead stop on the side of the road.

"Something wrong?"

The memories of the best winter day he'd ever had swept through his mind like a blizzard swept through a city. He never thought he'd go back.

For the longest time he was embarrassed to, having broken a promise to return. It was ridiculous, he knew, to think something he'd said at the age of ten could be held against him, but it stuck with him. Then the older he got the more reasons he had not to make the trip over.

He must have imagined going back millions of times. Thought of what it would be like to see Lee, the feisty, confident girl who'd held the place as his adolescent crush for more years than he'd like to admit.

Maybe that's why he'd never gone back? He knew he would notice her the instant he saw her. He knew, without having seen her, she would have grown into a beautiful woman.

"Jackson, did I lose you?"

"Sorry, no, I..." Had he told the old man his name? He couldn't remember. "I just, I've been there before."

"Oh great, so you know all about it."

"Well, it's been...wow," Jackson paused to rub a hand against a rough, chilled chin, "about twenty years."

"How great it will be to see it again. They do say absence makes the heart grow fonder."

Jackson eyed Nick, wondering if he was talking only of the farm? But how could he be talking of anything different.

Maybe he would take the day. Clear his mind.

"Sure. You said they needed help?"

"That I did."

"Then I'll see what I can do."

"Great! What a great day this is going to be."

CHAPTER 4

"What is happening today? Is *anything* going to go right?"

Finley let her head fall to the steering wheel of the hauling truck she was using to take trees down to the lot.

For a moment Blair simply stared from the other side of the truck door. This was the third piece of bad news she had delivered today, there wasn't much else to do besides let her cousin's distress take over. She knew it wouldn't last long, so she'd just wait it out.

"Okay," Finley began with her head still resting on the wheel, "you're covering for the shop girls who are out this afternoon. I'm covering for Blake to help Grandpa beginning at noon. And now you're telling me Santa Claus can't make it because he has the flu? Which, if my instincts are right, means he'll be out all season."

Blair didn't want to agree, but that pretty much nailed it. "Yes. So far." At the crane of Finley's neck and meeting the wide, *I can't believe you just said that,* eyes, Blair agreed she probably didn't need to add that last bit.

"Lee, we got this. We can figure it out. It's only ten. We've done a ton of work so far this morning. If the trees get thin we'll survive. Bobby can cut and haul. We can pull Miles from the kitchen if we need to. And how hard can it really be to find a Santa Claus at Christmas?"

"Okay, you've managed to give me the ounce of hope I needed. Hop in. Let's drive down, get this load of trees to the lot, and head to the office. We need to find a Santa."

One hour, seventy calls between them, and not a single Santa Claus was to be found. Apparently, during their earlier assessment, finding a Santa during Christmas was like finding ice in the desert. Between the 'Ma'am, you do realize it's Christmas?' questions and the humor they were met with on the other end of their calls, they found out pretty quickly.

They also noted, as the number of calls they made increased, so did the number of customers. As lunchtime neared, the paths were full, the tree lot was packed, and though she didn't want to see it, the line for visiting Santa was already starting to form.

"Blair?"

Blair looked up from her list of numbers, only three left to call, she noted, and followed Finley's line of sight to the workshop.

"Oh." The image registered and Blair wasn't feeling as optimistic as she had been.

"Do we still have the old Santa suit in storage?"

"Uh, the one that looks like–"

Finley wouldn't let her say it out loud. "Yes." The word was quick and sharp. "*That* one."

Even in the hectic situation Blair had to stifle the giggle that threatened to bubble out. "Ah, yes, we do."

Finley closed her eyes and nodded. "Let's go get it."

Without a word, Blair – who looked unnervingly pleased – jumped up to head to the farmhouse basement. The basement door creaked, echoing throughout the house, and the sound was enough to whisk Finley back to the last time they'd had to pull out *the suit.* Grandpa Chuck, as far as she knew, was the only one to ever have worn it.

Wearing it was a rite of passage that nobody wanted. On the few occasions it had been dragged from the trenches to make an appearance, nothing had gone right. The first year Grandpa Chuck's beard had been pulled off, the old down pillow he'd stuffed in his jacket popped, and they'd taken on a disbelieving group of teenagers that had destroyed the lives of the young children in the line that year who found out too early Santa Claus wasn't real.

And, Finley winced, those were the *good* bad days. The worst being the day Grandpa tripped while putting on the old suit and broke his foot. He refused to go to the hospital until the day with the kids was through – 'there will be a Santa!' Now, the thought had her lip lifting at the memory, then it wasn't so funny. That, and, the excuse that was used for the bum leg was Santa got run over by one of his reindeer – something else that didn't sit well with the children visiting the farm.

"Got it! Here it is." Blair hurried in showing off the long black garment bag, pulling Finley from her memories.

"If I didn't know any better I'd say you're excited about this?"

A hint of apology came and went from the young, pretty face. "No. Well, it's just that I've never *seen* it in action. I've only heard the stories. And of course, I don't want to see anything go wrong…"

Finley dropped her head and laughed. "Another kind of rite of passage I guess."

"Sorry, what?"

Left with no other options, Finley held out her hand for the garment bag and said, "Better go get Grandpa."

Ignoring the delighted squeal, the bag found her hand with a heavy plop. Before she could add instructions, the girl was gone.

Finley spoke to herself, "Okay, you go get grandpa, I'll call Bobby to see if he can stand in at the tree lot for a bit. No, no." Finley lifted a hand to no one. "It's okay, you go, I got it."

Sighing and making a mental note to find Maeve later and tell her how much she was *enjoying* the first day of the season, Finley looked outside and took in the reluctant moment.

She noticed nobody seemed to know they were short-staffed. Nobody realized they were a row of trees behind in the lot. It, all things considered, looked like people were having a good time just letting the Christmas season be upon them. There wasn't rushing or arguing. There wasn't, she saw, an unpleasant face in the crowd.

Scanning from the shops to Santa's workshop, she also saw somebody enjoying her hay bale. Looking, she supposed, just like she did when she found her way over there and got lost in her thoughts.

The man, she noted, sat with his back straight, hands folded on his lap, his head leaned back, and his eyes closed. He looked...content? No, she leaned closer to the window and focused, he looked resigned.

Well, she leaned back into her chair, she knew how that felt.

Right there with ya buddy.

CHAPTER 5

Nick wandered into the tree farm feeling giddy. Like a child on Christmas Eve.

His eyes twinkled and his smile beamed.

This time of year, he had to force himself to slow down, because if he didn't he'd get lost in the excitement. The simple sound of *Santa Claus is Comin' to Town* playing through the old-fashioned tuba-looking speakers was enough to distract him into singing along.

When they arrived, he let Jackson go ahead and let him know he was going to wander for a bit before tracking down the farm manager. Jackson didn't seem to mind so Nick took his time and started his admiration at the entrance.

A looming iron sign stood tall over the gravel path leading into the farm. It welcomed all of the excited guests, boasting beautifully, *Winter Haven Tree Farm*. The posts holding the sign were wrapped in green garland with those tiny little twinkle lights. What a sight they must have made as day turned into an early night.

The long path stretched for what seemed like a mile to the base of a hill that was home to acre upon acre of pine. On the left side of the path stood a glorious farmhouse. Windows and a front porch wrapped what looked like the entire circumference of the home, all outlined with the same greenery and lights. To the right, a row of shops sat side-by-side, each painted cranberry red with pretty white trim. Worn wooden signs with a touch of fresh paint hanging from the front of each building shared what people would find if they chose to wander inside.

Nick chuckled to himself, thrilled he'd get to spend the season at such a wonderful farm, it was such a place of happiness.

He continued his walk past one of the smaller buildings in the row that enticed not only with a brightly decorated half barn door, but with the smell of chocolate and buttery sugar cookies. The line was long with parents and children, groups of friends, and couples young and old, but it was moving quickly and efficiently. Nick thought about a quick detour, but decided he'd have more time after he settled in.

As Nick came around to the back side of the house he noticed Jackson sitting on a hay bale taking in the view, much as he just was. Nick's round cheeks lifted in a knowing smile, then he turned left toward a sign that let him know the farm's management offices were just around the corner.

"Hello, Sir? Can I help you?"

Nick swiveled toward the happy greeting and beamed when he found a young woman followed by an old man. She looked much more pleased than the fellow following her, but Nick supposed he could help with that.

"Well, hello there! I'm just passing by - for now. I was hoping I could speak to the manager, or perhaps owner of the farm? Whoever is in charge of this wonderful wonderland?"

"Sure, follow us. We are just heading in to see her now."

Nick had to pick up his pace a bit to keep up, but fell into step next to the young woman's frowning companion. "I'm Nick." He held out a hand.

"Nice to meet you, Nick. I'm in trouble. But most people around here just call me Grandpa Chuck. You can call me Chuck."

Nick hooted with laughter and let a delightful pat on Chuck's back. "It's very nice to meet you, too. Your granddaughter, I presume?"

Nodding, Chuck said, "We try to hide it but something about the same eyes, long stick of a body, and pretty much every other feature we have, gives us away. You think this one looks like me, you should see the one inside – the one you're looking for. To what do we owe the pleasure?"

"I happen to be looking for a job. I'm Santa Claus."

"Well!" Chuck's eyebrows rose in delight. "How about that? I might not be in so much trouble after all. And I might be saved a trip to the hospital this year. Yes. Yes, indeed. Follow us right in."

The house smelled of sweet cinnamon and a hint of orange. And somebody must have started a wood fire. How glorious. The inside matched the outside. Though it wasn't painted red, it held the same rustic charm as the grounds.

They walked through a set of glass-paned double doors, into an office where a woman, who could have been a twin to the young lady who ushered him in, was sitting and staring out the window.

"Lee?" The young lady began as the woman in the chair startled and spun around. "I have Grandpa Chuck and a nice gentleman who asked to see you. Are you available?"

The woman smiled, but Nick could see it was to cover up the worry of what he assumed meant to her another distraction.

"Yes, hello. Of course, I have time. How can I help you, Sir?" She motioned with her hand for Nick to take a seat.

"Why, thank you. I hope I'm not an inconvenience but I'm hoping to speak to you about a job."

He watched the woman look from the young to the old guests in the room. Chuck, he noted, was nodding and smiling.

"What type of a job are you looking for?"

"Well, I'm Santa Claus. I–"

"Your job is being Santa Claus?" The excitement flew out, along with a hint of hope.

Nick laughed, then watched the room and their astonishment at how much he not only looked like Santa, but that he sounded like him as well. His *ho-ho* was quite distinct.

"It is. And, I'm wondering if you have any other openings? I brought a friend with me today."

The young lady from behind him quipped not so untruthfully, "Is he a Jack-of-all-trades?"

"As a matter of fact, I believe he is. And his name is Jack, come to think of it. I've known only a couple Jack's in my life, one that causes a little mischief, but the rest have been quite agreeable."

"If he's a hard worker, we can pretty much work with anything. I'm Finley Whittaker. This is Blair, our farm's assistant manager. This is," Finley wondered how to introduce her grandfather, "this is—"

"A grateful Grandpa Chuck." He looked to Finley. "We've met. I like him already."

Finley's lips twitched. "You only like him because he's saving you from *the suit.*"

"With my track record he's saving me from a heck of a lot more than that."

"Well, Nick. I would give you a formal interview and check references but we are finding ourselves in a bit of a bind today. If you're available, how about we use today as your live interview and we can discuss what the rest of the season looks like at the end of the day?"

Nick rested his hands on his large belly and let it jiggle as he nodded happily. "Yes. Yes, I think that sounds quite good."

"Perfect! Now, what do you need as far as costume and equipment?"

"Oh, well, if it's all the same to you I'd like to wear my own. I can run it by you before I make my grand entrance to see if you approve. Though, I think you'll find it'll do the trick."

"Nick," Finley said while pushing off of her chair, "you couldn't be more of an answer to our prayers than if the real Santa rode in on his sleigh. Now, you said you had a friend named, Jack?"

"Jack!"

Jackson turned to see Nick pumping his arms down the path, then waving his hand to get his attention. He hopped off the hay bale, dusted off his pants and jacket, just in time to see her. When he did, he froze. He couldn't believe what he was seeing.

In an instant he was ten and following her around the farm having the best day of his life. Now here she was, standing right in front of him. He imagined she'd be beautiful, but what he couldn't have imagined was the way seeing her again would take his breath away. And his words.

"Jack," Nick said again, "this is Finley Whittaker. She's the owner of the farm and just so happens to need a *Jack* of all trades. I told her you might be her man."

After a moment Jack realized he hadn't said anything, just stared. Still unable to find words he decided on nodding repeatedly. He nodded from Finley to Nick, who gave him a bemused smile, before he realized he needed to pull it together.

"Ah, sorry. My manners got lost in the view." Jackson shifted, then motioned toward the hill of pines, then stretched out his hand. And because he didn't know if she remembered him or not, and because he wasn't sure if he was ready for her to remember, he said, "I'm Jack."

Finley's inquisitive look held as their hands shook. Maybe she was analyzing him, judging his weird behavior. Hopefully, he thought, she needed the help more than she was worried about having a crazy person around – since that's what he felt like he was being.

"Nice to meet you, Jack. What type of work can you do?"

"Right, work. I ah, well, just about anything. Retail," he said, nodding toward the buildings. "I can build, landscape, cut," he pointed to the hill, "operate machinery. Pretty much anything outdoors, I can do."

He watched her look him up and down, wondering if he was giving her a line. He couldn't blame her, seeing as he was dressed as though he stepped right out of a men's formal-wear catalogue. Maybe he should give her a little reassurance.

"I came with Nick kind of spur of the moment. I have proper work attire – for whatever you need me to do – at home. Depending on when you'd need me to start, I can be there and back within the hour, maybe sooner. I'm not too far from here."

Finley nodded, but said nothing. He watched her shift from one foot to the other, then put her gloved hands on her hips. Jack grinned at the gloves, having never forgotten them. He guessed they weren't the same ones she wore all those years ago, but he appreciated the tradition.

"Okay then."

"Okay?" Jackson felt what must be excitement. It was the first time he'd felt that way in years. It should probably be a feeling of dread, seeing as he just took a job here when he should be figuring what in the heck to do about his family business. But it didn't seem to stop him from accepting.

"Okay," Finley confirmed, then looked at her watch. "Let's see, it's almost noon now. Do you think you could be back by one?"

"Yes, ah–"

It wasn't until that moment Jackson realized he didn't have his car.

"Yes, yes." Nick jumped in. "We rode together. He'll use my car and be back before you even knew he was gone."

"Great. Then let's get started, shall we?" Finley said, with a look that was more thankful than concerned.

Jack thanked Nick when he handed him the keys to his car, then watched the two of them walk away. There were a million things he should probably be concerned about at the moment, but the only thing that came to his mind was that she hadn't recognized him.

He didn't know if he was thankful, or feeling forgotten. Which was stupid. How could he expect that from her after only a day together, twenty Christmases ago?

Unable to feel sorry for himself for too long due to the buzzing of his phone coming from his pocket, Jack pulled it out and saw the readout. He should have known he was gone too long. Jake would be burning a hole in the office carpet by now waiting on his return. He didn't want to answer, but he knew he'd only be making it worse for himself.

When he slid his finger across the phone, he didn't answer, just lifted the phone to his ear.

"Where are you?" Jake's voice was stern, not leaving room for pleasantries.

Jackson looked around at what used to be his favorite place in the world, and decided he was going to do something for himself. What he was about to say wasn't a lie. It was just a simple way for his brother to misunderstand his intentions.

"I'm working on something."

"Good. Report back to me when you have it together."

"It will take a couple weeks." Jackson heard the annoyed sigh thunder as it whooshed through the phone.

"Fine, but it better be good. We need this."

He thought about responding, but was greeted with a dial tone that told him their call was over. Then, the funniest thing happened. He felt something he hadn't in a long, long time: happiness.

CHAPTER 6

Finley had forgotten she hadn't seen Nick before he was put to work. That meant she wasn't able to give him the once-over before approving his suit. She'd been called to the tree lot to help and wasn't able to make it back due to the after-lunch rush. Surprisingly, she felt OK about it.

Feeling like she was being pulled in two directions, Blair stepped up and told her not to worry about it, that she had it covered. Rather than be concerned, Finley felt reassured – thankful even – to have the extra set of hands. Then she wasn't given a second to dwell on it.

From the moment she walked into the lot she was hit with the scent of pine and a swarm of customers - she was swamped. She helped a family of five pick out a ten-foot tree because the parents of the three young children couldn't say no to the amazed, wide eyes. She laughed when Grandpa Chuck bet her ten bucks they'd have to cut the top off to make it fit in their living room. She helped a cute older couple pick out a small tree that the lady said would sit on their side table, just as it had since they moved into their townhome. Another newlywed couple who didn't so much care about the tree as much as holding hands while walking around the lot, sipping hot chocolate and snapping endless amounts of pictures.

The time escaped her. Finley realized she got lost in the people, listened to their stories, watched them, and found herself smiling as she did.

When was the last time she had worked in the lot for hours without thinking of the next task? Not in five years she guessed. She'd have to thank Nick and Jack for quite literally showing up unannounced right when she needed them, giving her the time to breathe.

"You're off somewhere. First time I've seen you drift since you walked in today. Must be some kind of record."

Finley grinned at her grandpa who was looking on dotingly. Like she and her dad, she and her grandpa shared a special bond. The farm, after all, had passed from grandpa, to mom and dad, to her.

"I had a good day today." Finley leaned her hip on the side of the wooden stand that was used to accept payment for the trees.

"Day doesn't seem to be over yet."

The gleam in her grandpa's eye had her smiling again. "And just what are you getting at, old man?"

"I might be old and you might be having a good day, but that doesn't mean you don't want to go make sure everything is running according to schedule. You might want to go micromanage your new grounds man, too. See how well he's working out. Looked good in those jeans he came back in."

"You," Finley pointed at her grandpa while the amusement on her face grew, "are a troublemaker."

But, she did happen to catch Jack walking back in, then as he stood and listened intently while taking orders from Blair. She had to admit, the jeans didn't hurt the already tall, dark, and handsome man. Something else about him was compelling, too. She felt pulled to him. She supposed it's what had her inclined to trust him. That and desperation.

"Doesn't mean you aren't thinking about it."

Now her grandpa was being downright obnoxious, especially with the knowing, teeth-baring smile he was wearing due to catching her in another daydream.

"For your information, though I shouldn't even have to share, I was just thinking something about him seems familiar. Though, with all the traffic we get year after year that's really no surprise."

"Oh, yeah. You're absolutely right. That's *exactly* why he looks good in those jeans."

Lifting her hip, Finley stalked over to her grandpa who had taken rest on the tall stool behind the counter, gave him a swift peck on the side of his head, and said, "For that, I am leaving you to fend for yourself."

Before getting too far, she turned. "But, if you need help, call me."

Earning a wink, she continued out of the lot. Time to spy on Santa Claus.

It was just after four, but the winter dusk was upon them. It wouldn't be long and the farm would be lit only by twinkle lights and amber lamps. People were everywhere, but the crowd at this time of the day didn't matter, it still felt quiet. Maybe it was the cold, maybe the dark, or maybe the quick dusting of snow they were receiving, but it was peaceful.

Finley breathed in her surroundings and let out a little laugh at the way the day had played out.

Not over yet, her mind warned.

But it turned out well enough so far for her to appreciate the moment.

As she neared Santa's workshop, what was quiet and peaceful outside, sounded like a war on the inside. The screaming and yelling had her footsteps quickening as she rushed toward the room full of casualties.

Before she knew it, she was moving at a run to get inside, panic rising with every step while punishing herself for calling it a good day before it was over. When she pulled open the door and turned the corner toward Santa's chair, Blair caught her arm, stopping her in an instant. Finley looked over wildly, startled by the grip.

When Blair did nothing but smile and lift a finger from the hand that was holding a clipboard to her mouth suggesting silence, Finley obeyed then followed Blair's eyes.

Moving her head toward the sound, what she saw wasn't screams or shouting, but cheering and singing. As if on cue, all of the kids and their parents threw their arms in the air, counted to three as a mass, then waved their hands from side to side as they sang along to *Jingle Bells.*

"What is going on?" Finley whispered to Blair where they were standing out of sight.

"He's amazing, that's what's going on." Blair's words were pure admiration. "The line was *huge* by the time he dressed and was ready to come out. I got maybe a minute to check out the suit before I had no choice but to give him the green light. But, as you can see, I didn't need more than ten seconds because his suit is the best I've ever seen."

Blair paused so they both could try and see through the laughter and movement to get a better look at the man in red. When Finley caught a glimpse she only lifted an intrigued brow and nodded her agreement. It was good, really, *really* good.

"Anyway," Blair continued, "the line's huge. He comes out and instantly all of the kids settle down. The man has an aura. They stare at him in literal wonder. Then he starts going through the kids one by one, laughing with them, talking about their favorite Christmas activities, everything. He's taking time, but moving through the line fast. He's brilliant. Then the kids start to get a little restless, and before I know it he's got everybody singing frickin' Christmas carols – even the crabby parents."

"I think he might be the real Santa."

Both of the women jumped at the unfamiliar voice that snuck up behind them to offer input.

"Whoa." Jackson jumped at their surprised reaction. "Sorry, didn't mean to startle you. I was heading to find some water and heard all of the commotion. Wanted to check on Nick seeing as this is his domain. From the looks of it he has everything under control and more. Do you think he's using magic?"

Now the women shared a smile and turned back.

"Whatever he's using is fine by me. Looks like he's got a full-time gig if he wants it." Finley turned to face Jack, not having realized earlier how tall he was, she looked up to meet his face. "Mind if we make the rounds to see if you get the same good grade?"

Jackson saw her guard waver just a bit before she got down to business. At least he wasn't the only one that was flustered. Though for him it had more to do with finding a long-lost crush than anything else. Which, now that he thought it, sounded completely ridiculous. But that didn't stop him from wanting to see her as he came down from the hill with loads of trees to replenish and scraps to drop off at the wreath shop.

Loads of trees. Crap, he thought. He better get back up there. But, water. Right, he came for water. And now she was going with him. Right. It took him a minute to get his thoughts in order.

"Sounds good to me," he finally answered. "Mind if we try and find that water? I think Bobby would be just as, if not more grateful, than me. I already feel sore and I haven't had a chance to sleep on it to make it worse."

Finley's easy laugh was like Christmas music to his ears. "The first couple of days can do that to you. I suggest a couple aspirin and a lot of that water you're requesting. If you'd ask Grandpa Chuck, or my dad, they'd advise a jar full of Apple Pie."

Finley led the way to the bakery where they'd find the water, and saw the confusion when she looked back to see if Jack was keeping stride.

"You eat apple pie out of a jar? And it helps with sore muscles?"

Finley couldn't help but brighten as she spoke. "Oh, you've not been introduced to our kind of Apple Pie, I see. Well, we'll have to acquaint you. And you better make sure Nick is driving. Or you're sticking around for a while."

"Now I'm intrigued."

"Let's start you off with water and see how you hold up through the rest of the night."

He swore her eyes twinkled as she spoke, or maybe he needed the water more than he knew. But he saw the young girl he'd met all those years ago still inside of her.

When they swung the door open to the bakery he thought he might have died and gone to heaven. Christmas candy and sweets, heaven. He circled the room and saw hard candies swirled with reds and greens, bags of homemade caramels and fudge, pretzels dipped in white and dark chocolates, and behind the counter, what he assumed was an endless supply of every Christmas cookie in the world.

"If you ever need help in here, I'm your man."

"You'll have to fight the entire staff to get yourself first in that line."

Finley walked to the counter and waited for Maeve to hand two oversized gingerbread men to a boy and girl who couldn't have been older than five and seven.

"On second thought, I better not. I'd see faces like those and forget they had to pay for anything. Free gingerbread for everybody!" He grinned and snuck a glance at an amazed Finley.

"To what do I owe the pleasure of my best friend and what looks like a new member of the team? You've been up with Bobby."

Jackson looked down wondering what she saw that he didn't, aside from his aching legs.

Maeve let out a hoot and winked at Finley who was rolling her eyes. She waved her hand and explained. "Just kidding, Jack. Blair was in here hours ago giving us the farm gossip. Seems we got Santa and a helper all in one shot today. She also let me know that if you came in here and needed anything that it wasn't some cute guy just trying to get a handout."

"I'm back to my original offer," Jackson said, looking to Finley again, "I'd like to work in here."

His comment earned him another laugh as a tall and muscular man walked to the front with a fresh tray of sugar cookie cutouts. This particular batch were expertly decorated to look like Santa's reindeer.

The man spoke up as he set the tray down. "Is she hitting on the new staff again?" Miles directed his question to Finley, ignoring the adoring look his wife was sending his way.

"She is. Can't control this one. It's a good thing you tied her down early."

"Don't I know it." Miles shifted to the left and leaned over the counter. "Miles Booker, Mrs. Booker's generously patient husband."

"Jack." *Just* Jack, he reminded himself. He reached the rest of the way across the counter to shake Miles's hand. "Jack Bloom. If you ever want to trade places let me know. I'm an expert cookie tester. Though, everything before the testing part is a little shaky."

Finley watched the exchange and appreciated how easy Jack was with her friends. That was important when the staff of such a large operation was so small.

"We don't suppose we can get a couple waters from you? And," Finley didn't often give in, but it was Maeve that told her to enjoy the work, and testing cookies could be considered just that, "maybe a couple cookies. You know, for testing, and *enjoyment.*"

"For you two, anything."

Maeve moved quickly as Miles began helping the next customers in line, not missing her own words used back at her. In seconds she had waters and three cookies wrapped and ready to go.

"Here you go. Jack, if you need real food, head straight through that door. That's where we keep the pastries, sandwiches, soups, and more. I might be biased but I think just about everything in there hits the mark."

"She's not lying. Do you need a meal?"

"I can't wait to try it, but for now I better get back up to Bobby. Thanks, Maeve."

Maeve stood with her hands on her hips as she watched the two walk out. When Finley looked back before walking out the door, she mouthed, *He is dreamy!* It earned her a brush off and a grin, which told her Finley agreed.

It only took ten minutes to eat their cookies, decide they were the best they've ever had, and reach Bobby right where Jackson had left him. It left little room for small talk, but after the day he had, and he supposed Finley had too, it was nice to enjoy the starlit ride up.

"I thought maybe you'd gone and skipped out on me." Bobby Mills stood as the truck slowed to a stop and Finley and Jackson hopped out.

"I only thought about it twice, both times my muscles screamed at me as I climbed in and out of the truck." Jackson appreciated the comradery and the friendly chuckle he'd gotten out of Bobby. "To make it up to you, the boss worked out a deal at the bakery."

Jackson tossed the water over first, then walked the rest of the way to hand over the homemade cookie.

"A hand-off like this makes me feel like I can hardly complain. Ready to get back at it in a few?"

"Point me in the direction you need me."

Bobby shifted to his right and nodded down the row. "See the saw about fifteen trees down?"

"I do."

"Let's start there and work our way over. Let's bring down another two dozen, we'll take inventory on drop off, and see what sizes we need for the next load."

Finley watched the men interact. It seemed so natural. They've already found a good system, and it looked to be working for both of them. She watched as Jack pulled on old work gloves with wear holes on the pads of their palms and on some of the fingers. They looked stiff with lack of use, but perhaps that explained the fancy suit and jacket he'd shown up in.

When he looked over to her before he walked away, it could have been the most natural thing in the world. The way he simply nodded, grinned, then turned to head back to work. But the way his eyes held hers, like they wanted to get one more look at her before they had to leave, bore into her.

Finley felt her belly do a little flip, and her mind wondered again if she'd seen him before. Then the moment swiftly ended with embarrassment as Bobby pulled her out of her thoughts.

"What do you think of our new guy?"

"He's – ah – he seems like he," Finley stuttered searching for words that help her awkward recovery, "is a little rusty. But overall, seems like he holds his own." Good, she thought, that's good. "That's actually what I came up to ask you. How's it going so far?"

Bobby scratched his head through his stocking cap and grinned. He wouldn't give her too hard of a time. She'd had a day. "Your assessment is pretty good."

Both of their gazes shifted to Jackson who was efficiently moving from one tree to the next. "You're right, he is rusty. But what he's shaking off in rust he makes up for with hard work. I like him.

Didn't realize how much I liked him until he made the job a heck of a lot easier. Two sets of hands up here are better than one."

Finley agreed, then said, "I think that settles it then. Looks like if he wants it, you'll have some full-time help around here for the season. We'll pull him from time to time when we need it, but other than that, he's yours."

"I'll take what I can get. Thanks, Lee."

Bobby pushed up from the back of his own truck where he had sat when they pulled up and tried for one more poke. "I'll head over to help so you can have a little more time to ogle him in private."

Finley's head snapped to Bobby's and his heavy laugh filled the space between them.

"I was not, and do not, *'ogle.'*" She stood a little straighter and let her eyes slide to Jack momentarily before directing her words to Bobby again. "I merely appreciate good work when I find it – or in this case – is gifted to me by Santa Claus."

"Mm-hmm. You must have been *really* good this year."

Finley couldn't help her laugh as Bobby joined Jack to continue their work. She wasn't the type to stew, and definitely wouldn't hang on Bobby's words, so for now she would just graciously accept that if she was given Jack for having a good year, she'd take it.

The double-feature had started on the big screen and Finley couldn't believe they'd made it through the day. She stood back, watching the crowd cuddle together, eyes glued to the boy on the screen as he turned his house into a party and danced to *Jingle Bell Rock*.

Looking around she saw the buildings start to empty, people who weren't quite ready to leave wandering toward the movie, or making their way to the parking lot. She looked through the window of the bakery as Nick sat with Maeve and Miles, all taking a well-deserved break to indulge in some of their handiwork. Blair sent her a quick wave as she made her way into the wreath-making building, most likely to check on supplies. And much like her friends and Nick were doing, Bobby, her grandpa, and Jack were all sharing a laugh huddled around the lot stand, pausing their commotion only when a customer found them to pay or join in.

Finley folded her arms for warmth and comfort, and leaned on the lamppost as she took it all in.

The snow had stopped, but that didn't make the night any less beautiful. It had been dark for hours already, but she decided she liked that about winter. She supposed she always had, but something about tonight, about the way everything looked when she stood back and took it all in, had her appreciating it, noticing it.

Time had passed easily as she stood there. She should probably be working on something, but decided whatever it was could wait. Or, until Blair found her to let her know she was needed. When she saw Blair again, the young woman had her clipboard in hand talking to Jack. She was pointing to her agenda and smiling, while Jack looked on intently, offering understanding nods. The two exchanged a handshake, a sign to Finley that Blair had delivered the news they'd like him to stay on for the season, and Blair sped away toward the farm house.

Finley smiled at Jack as he stretched his muscles and let it linger as he stood with his hands on his hips and did a little spin taking everything in. She couldn't help but notice the change in him throughout the day. He seemed different in such a short time.

She didn't see the contemplating man in the suit sitting on the hay bales. She saw an overworked man, satisfied and appreciative. And for the first time in a long time she'd seen something she hadn't in years, what it looked like – what she imagined she looked like once – when you loved what you were doing.

CHAPTER 7

The morning came early, it came dark, and it came with screaming muscles throughout his body. But the time and the aches weren't enough to dim his excitement for the day ahead.

Jackson laid in bed for only a moment to wonder if it was the work or the woman that was pushing him out from his warm comforter into the cold that seeped in overnight.

Twenty years of wondering about a woman, dreaming of her. The job was good, he supposed, but he'd put all his money on it being the woman's doing.

Not just any woman. *Finley,* he thought.

It had caught him off guard when they'd been reintroduced. Of course, she didn't know that, but he had expected the innocent, *'I'm Lee,'* he'd gotten as a child. Instead, it was…what was it? More formal? Less child-like? Less fun? Less wonder?

He tried to pinpoint it the day before, but he couldn't quite get a good grasp on what had changed. Finley was still magnificent in his mind, but the woman who had stood in front of him, kept a close eye on him, had lost a bit of her energy, the joy he'd once seen.

Jackson flung the comforter off and stood, letting the chill take away the last bit of weariness. Then he thought, if she lost the spark he'd fallen for all those years ago, he'd just have to find a way to get it back. It had only been a single day, but he decided the moment he laid eyes on Finley Whittaker again, he wasn't going to miss another Christmas with her.

After a quick shower, a home-brewed coffee to go, and leaving the store-bought donuts on the counter, Jackson strolled out the door. He had a couple things to do that morning. He needed new work clothes, and he needed to work up an appetite to use at Maeve and Miles's bakery.

But, first things first. He jumped in his jeep and steered toward his family's outfitter in town, and for the heck of it tuned the radio into the local Christmas station. He might be listening to holiday jingles all day long but he found he was in the spirit.

"Well, well. Look at you." Maeve applauded his appearance when she looked up and saw him walking through the door. Miles offered a whistle that had them laughing and Jack doing a quick spin to show off his new work-wear.

"You almost look like you belong here. By the end of the day I'm sure you'll dirty up a bit and fit right in."

"That's what I'm hoping for. But before I do that, I've got breakfast on my mind. Can talk you into serving me up? I even skipped my daily donut."

"If you're not careful you'll start skipping the rest of your at-home meals, too. And you'll start looking like me." Miles patted his belly with one hand as he cleaned the last of the tables with the other.

"It's a risk I am willing to take."

"That's what I like to hear. What can I get you?"

"I saw a ham and cheese croissant on the menu yesterday. And a chocolate scone. I don't suppose you could ring me up for both."

"Oh yeah, you're a goner."

"You just ignore him, it's coming right up."

Jackson eyed his watch and saw it was coming up on six-thirty. He was anxious to get started, but he was glad to have the time to sit and enjoy the farm - especially the warm bakery - before it was swarming with people. He figured the next two days would be like the last and it probably wouldn't slow down until the weekdays hit.

"Here you go, sweetie. Anything else?"

He shook his head. "No, this is perfect. Everything about it is perfect."

"You're right, Miles, he might be a goner."

"I was a goner a long time ago."

Jackson didn't know where it came from or what made him say it out loud. He hadn't intended on bringing it up, and definitely didn't feel like it was the right time to tell Finley. But he saw the mischief in Maeve's eyes and knew from the curious look on her face he wasn't going to get out of sharing it with her.

"I had a feeling about you." Maeve admitted as she slowly walked up to his table and slid into the chair across from him. "I'm wondering if I'm right."

"I suppose it depends on what you think you know." Though he figured she knew exactly if she and Finley had been friends as long he'd been pining for a long lost ten-year-old.

"Why don't you try me, *Jackson.*"

Ah, there it was. The defeated grin fell across his face and he knew she knew. So, he settled in, took a bite of his hot breakfast, then started talking.

The story wasn't long, or full of twists and turns. He hadn't been kept away by blizzarding winter weather or life-altering Christmas moments. His family just simply hadn't returned. Like you'd visit a restaurant or shop once, and for no reason at all, never quite make it back. Though he remembered the years following his visit like they were yesterday. Endlessly begging his parents to go back. But slowly, the older he got, the more embarrassed he felt.

The last time he asked his parents to go to Winter Haven his brothers, even his younger brother, had given him grief for weeks. And by the next year, even if he had asked, he didn't know if he wanted to go. What if Finley – *Lee* – didn't remember him, recognize him, or worse, didn't want to see him at all?

61

"So," Jackson looked at Maeve and Miles, who were now both sitting across from him, all work paused, hanging on every word, "the years passed, I would wait for another Christmas to come and go, thinking about stopping by just to wander, but never quite convincing myself to come."

Jackson paused to take another bite and shake his head unable to believe how he'd finally made it back. "Then, out of nowhere, Nick picks me out of a crowd and offers me his extra coffee. Before you know it I'm in a car with a guy who looks a heck of a lot like Santa Claus and I'm on my way over to offer a helping hand at Winter Haven."

Maeve's dreamy sigh came before her words. "It's fate."

"It's something, alright." Jackson could admit that much, but *fate* might be pushing it. "There is one thing…"

Jackson stopped, not sure how to broach the subject.

Miles leaned back and sipped his own coffee. "You won't be able to get away with those half sentences here." Then he nodded to Maeve and let Jackson take in her determined expression.

"You might as well spit it out, because one way or another, I'll get it out of you." Maeve nodded only a single time, as if it meant her words were final and she wouldn't take no for an answer.

Jackson could only give a half-laugh and get on with it. "She – Lee – Finley, you know? She seems…well, I don't even know how to explain it. Less joyful?"

When he looked up their facial expressions didn't change so he tried for more. "I know, that sounds ridiculous. But I remember that day like it was yesterday. It wasn't just the moment that was magical, not just the season, *she's* what I remember. Not Santa Claus, not the trinkets we bought, or the movies we watched. Sure, I'd never seen a place like this before, with sleigh rides and all, but as – I can't believe I'm saying this – *enchanting* as it all was, it would have been nothing without her."

Maeve didn't intend to give away her best friends' feelings, but she didn't want Jackson walking away empty handed either. Not after a homerun explanation like that. But if her instincts were right, he wasn't the same boy either.

"I'm not going to speak for Finley, her feelings are hers to share. But, if you ask me, you might not be feeling too differently than she is. Just sharing a quick observation is all."

"Observing is right."

The table full of heads exchanged guilty glances when they saw Finley standing in the doorway.

"How much of that did you hear?" Maeve couldn't help but ask.

"How much of it should I have heard?" Finley walked over, intrigued. She wished she could pretend she heard more than the last few words, but she'd spoken up too soon.

"Well, since you caught us, I suppose there's not much more we can explain. But I could try and butter you up with some cookies and coffee?"

Finley pointed a finger at Maeve as she walked over. "You know I'm weak. That and Blair downed over half the coffee before I even stepped foot into the kitchen this morning." She lifted her thermos. "I'm almost empty. If you fill it up and sweet talk me with a snickerdoodle, I might forget I heard a word."

Miles jumped out of his chair and swiped the thermos knowing when to take a good deal. And it helped him leave the scene. He was about as good at lying as Jack Frost was at bringing summer.

"What's on your agenda today?" Maeve said, changing the subject.

"Seems Jack and I had the same idea. Get over here early to enjoy a bit of the morning before we opened." Finley turned her attention to Jackson. "Since you are, maybe we could tour the grounds. Get you acquainted with all of our operations and staff so you have an idea of the things you'll be doing and the people you'll be lending a hand."

"Sounds great to me," Jackson said, satisfied he'd played it cool enough seeing as he'd been staring at Finley since she walked in.

Her clothes were the same as they had been twenty years earlier, but the way he saw her in them was different. The worn jeans hugged close to her body, the red flannel work shirt flowed around her trim top, and her ragged boots looked as if she could go for a winter ride on horseback or shovel an ice-rink. And her face; her face was different.

Jackson realized his years of imagining what she would look like when she was no longer a young girl had been wasted time. Because every image he conjured couldn't have described the woman he was seeing today. Her chocolate-colored eyes were framed by arched brows that matched her dark hair. Her mouth was wide and full, just a bit too big for her face. And the round of her cheeks and the slant of bone they sat on had deepened, matured. She was no longer a child, but a beautiful, captivating woman.

As he watched her walk out before him he paused at a feeling, something inside of him that was telling him he wouldn't be able to walk away again. And if any new promises were made, he'd have to keep them.

Jackson hovered in the doorway, shifting his weight from one foot to another, and turned to see Maeve and Miles staring after him.

"Can we just, you know, keep this between us for now?"

Maeve didn't like it, but it wasn't her place to interfere with her friend's life, or with Jackson's, who she realized she was pretty fond of already.

"For now. But she deserves to know. And you deserve it, too. It's been a long time."

Jackson nodded, letting the reality of the years rush through him. "Too long," he admitted. Then he smiled, and continued to walk out, following Finley, hoping they could find whatever they were looking for together.

Finley glanced over and grinned at the giddy, goofy smile Jack had plastered on his face. Before she realized what was happening she let out a little giggle and tried to stifle it so she wouldn't be caught. She didn't even make it to the end of the gravel road that would take them around to the new cabins – the first stop on their tour – before she was questioned.

"Is something funny?" Jackson asked. He liked having an excuse to look at her again.

"No, no. Not at all." Finley laughed again when their eyes met, then quickly diverting them.

"Okay, what is it? I have whipped cream on my face, don't I?" Jackson let himself feel the embarrassment – the humor – and self-consciously wiped his mouth with his shirtsleeve. He decided hearing Finley laugh was worth any self-deprecation.

"You just look so – so, like a kid at Christmas."

Finley turned toward the cabins and found Jack amazed once more.

"Wow." His eyes lit up and scanned the winter horizon.

Just over the cabins, to the east of the pine-filled hills, was a pink and orange sunrise. He'd seen many before, but this one caused the snow-covered ground to sparkle, and beams of sunlight to cascade through the bare, leafless trees that surround the farm. Smoke from chimneys puffed white clouds into the cold air from the cabins, making the view seem surreal. Like they were in their very own Christmas painting – one that would have been the picture on a puzzle his family would have put together when he was young.

"Can you believe you get to see this every day?"

Finley stared at the view and took in Jack's simple question. It really was beautiful. Was this what it looked like every morning? Or were other mornings different? If they were, did they offer their own kind of wonder?

"Yeah, I guess I do." Finley looked at Jack as if to study him in the same way he studied the skyline, then back again. "It really is pretty, isn't it?"

It was Jackson's turn to watch Finley take in the view. "Yes. The most beautiful thing I've ever seen."

Though, he wasn't sure if he was talking about the winter skyline, or her.

CHAPTER 8

Finley finished the morning having more fun than she'd expected. It turns out Jack not only loved the farm but was just as happy to have a good time while working on it.

After she watched Jack and Bobby exchange a secret handshake, one they must've come up with in about five minutes considering their lack of coordination, she looked on as Jack walked between the rows of trees before he began to make a row of cuts. She felt her head tilt and her breath sigh as he bobbed a finger on the top of a pine limb just to see the snow fly of the branch in glittery white sparkles. His actions had her doing the same before she turned to walk back to her truck. Their last stop of orientation was complete, and Jack was now stationed where he would start his day of work.

By the time she made it back to the bakery, she'd put in a couple hours in the wreath shop and helped Blair organize Santa's workshop before the afternoon session started.

Finley swung the door open and felt herself bounce in, earning an interested eyebrow from Maeve who was setting a steaming mug of warm-something on the bar counter and calling for *Sandy!*

Moving toward the register Finley asked along the way, "Did you happen to see the sunrise this morning?"

"I wasn't under the impression you knew the sun rose on the farm?" Maeve smiled her way to Finley.

"Ha-ha. Very funny." Finley grinned, squinting her eyes at Maeve. "I notice many things, but for some reason the sunrise this morning was," *what had Jack said?* "beautiful."

Leaning her hip on the counter, Maeve didn't respond. She simply crossed her arms and let her stare do the talking.

"Uh oh." Miles walked in and saw *the stance,* then nodded toward Finley. "Looks like you're in for it. What'd you do?"

Pretending to be offended, Finley defended herself and said, "I've done nothing but notice the beauty of the morning, thank you very much!"

"Oh." It was all Miles said.

"See?" Maeve said, satisfied with his agreement.

"Ok, you can't just say 'Oh' and 'See' and expect the rest of us to understand your one-word love language."

Finley paused for a moment to look at the board to place her order when new customers came in.

"Ham and cheese, hot chocolate, add mallows."

"Interesting." Maeve entered the meal into the register and charged it to the farm.

Scowling, Finley moved over, whispering, "I'll deal with you in a second."

Maeve happily took orders from a growing lunch crowd before she was able to return to Finley's *dealings.*

"Now, you were saying?" Maeve led off while handing her a white paper bag and festive to-go cup.

"Thank you." Finley took her lunch, then continued, "Though I don't see what's so interesting about my lunch order. Or, why noticing the sunrise is such a cause for surprise."

"Nothing really, except your order resembles what our handsome new farmhand ordered this morning. And I think the beauty in the sunrise might have more to do with that same handsome man than with Mother Nature."

"Oh, *come on.* You're projecting. I've ordered a ham and cheese croissant before."

"Last year."

"And, I've appreciated and talked about the farm."

"If you mean by grunting about how cold it's been, or how thick the snow is, or as I recall, just a couple days ago how you felt 'it's a burden'…then yes, you've '*talked about the farm.*'"

Finley cringed. "It's been that bad, huh?"

"Worse. You used to *love* this place. And today is the first time in years I've seen you smile for no reason and recognize the simple beauty of what you and your family have. It's refreshing. So, whether or not it's because of Jack, or just *because,* I'll take it. But I have my opinions."

"Well, you can have them. But maybe I'm just heeding the advice from my dearest friend and enjoying the season."

"I'd take that, too. Ok, now get out of my hair, I've got people to feed and satisfied smiles to create."

"Yeah, yeah." Finley waved a hand behind her as she walked out. "Talk to you later."

Jack parked the big truck he used to haul trees down to the lot after his last load. It was time for lunch and he was famished. When was the last time he felt hungry because of good old-fashioned hard work? Since the days of high school basketball and lacrosse he supposed. And then it probably didn't count since he was hungry all the time anyway.

He slammed the red door and walked around the back of the truck, patting the wooden boards that framed the back end of the trailer. He might just love this truck. Heavy duty, but had an old, solid feel to it.

Sliding off his gloves he started toward the bakery when Finley and Blair caught his eye. They talked for a minute then parted, Finley toward the front of the farmhouse and Blair toward the offices in the back. The urge to follow Finley was strong, but the need to get to Blair at the moment was stronger. And he could grab lunch on his way back up if he really needed to.

He shuffled his boots and did a little skip in the direction of the offices, while taking a deep breath of fresh air. Now *that* felt good. Without looking down, he felt the buzzing of his phone and pulled it out, then answered with a chipper, "Hello, it's a beautiful day!"

"I wish it was."

Jackson's face fell and his momentum slowed at the sound of his brother's voice.

"Jake, to what do I owe the pleasure?" He didn't intend to be irritated but his brother's tone immediately ruined his mood.

"The pleasure? Is that what you think I'm calling with? Dad just told me that you're taking time off?"

"No, I'm working on something that will keep me out of the office for a week or two. I believe I shared that information with you."

Though, Jackson thought, *hopefully it would be a heck of a lot more than two weeks.* But he decided to keep that much to himself.

"I didn't realize you'd be MIA from our offices. Care to share?"

"Not at the moment."

An exasperated sigh huffed through the phone and Jackson closed his eyes. He knew he was putting his brothers in a tough spot but he really would try and think of something. He just needed a break. And after being at the farm and realizing how rejuvenated he felt, he needed it more than he knew. He *felt* happy for the first time in years. Besides, a lot of people took time off during the holidays.

Now, whether that happiness was due to the farm or a woman, was yet to be determined. Either way, he'd take it.

"I know, Jake. I'm putting you in a tough spot. But please, trust me on this. Let me have this time." Because he needed it to come up with *something.*

"Okay, but in two weeks I'm reaching out again. And if there's nothing, we are going to sit down and figure something out."

"You have my word. And hey?"

"Yeah?"

"Try and enjoy a bit of the season."

The breathy laugh Jackson heard told him his brother hadn't completely lost all hope.

"Right, you too."

The click couldn't come soon enough, but he had to admit, the call didn't go as badly as he anticipated either. It was Jackson's turn to take a deep breath. Then, considering he had his two-week window, he started toward the offices once more listening to the happy crunching sound his work boots made on the snow-covered gravel path.

When he knocked, Blair looked up from a file she quickly closed and offered a smile. "Hey Jack, how's it going?"

"It's going great. Really great."

"That's, well, really great to hear. Is there something I can do for you?"

"Actually, yeah. During my orientation ride along I noticed your last cabin was empty. Any chance it's going to stay that way for a bit?"

Blair gave him a sideways grin and responded, "Actually, it's empty because the family that intended to stay had to back out last minute. They fill up quickly but usually in the summer months when people are planning ahead. The closer we get to Christmas the harder it will be to fill since people have already made their plans. Why do you ask?"

Ten minutes later Jackson was booked – at an employee discounted rate – for the next two weeks in the rustic little cabin that sat at the base of the hill next to rows of never-ending pine trees. His next stop was to see Nick – or, Santa Claus – to share the exciting news.

Jackson found it strange that he felt compelled to tell him, but he supposed it was a way of saying *thanks* since it was Nick who brought him back to the farm in the first place. He'd enjoy hearing the news.

Then, he thought as he heard his stomach rumble, he'd get some much-needed lunch.

CHAPTER 9

Finley raced down the stairs the next morning, dressed and ready for another day. She dashed into the kitchen, rushed over to the coffee pot, and watched the last drops of the pot trickle out into her cup.

"Already empty," she said, chuckling to herself, then replaced the empty pot, not bothering to make another. "Blair, your ambition is admirable, but I'll get you tomorrow."

Finley smiled at the little game she was playing – knowing full-well Blair had no idea Finley was trying to beat her to the kitchen to enjoy a fresh cup of coffee before it was gone.

Then, like she always did, she grabbed her hat, mittens, and jacket, threw them on and ran across the path to the bakery. Like she could count on her overzealous niece beating her to coffee, she could count on the bakery for a fresh latte and a delectable Danish.

With closed eyes, Finley inhaled deeply upon opening the door. Sugar, butter, yeast, and coffee. And just *smell that!* Was that cinnamon?

"It's perfection, right?"

Finley opened her eyes to see Jack sitting at a table with a view of the farm, looking at her with bright eyes and admiration. His look was contagious and she couldn't help the smile that formed through the surprise.

"Absolutely, perfect. You're up early again."

"Same time as yesterday. But today, I'm a resident."

"Oh?"

Maeve walked over to the table with a mug of hot chocolate and marshmallows, a paper cup of coffee, and a donut with white frosting and a mountain of red and green sprinkles. As she set the order down she said, "You're looking at the newest inhabitant of cabin number ten." Then Maeve slipped a sly smile toward Finley. "Anything I can get you this morning?"

Finley heard Maeve's spoken words and the look that said, *besides this handsome man?*

Not willing to admit her reaction was both surprise and excitement, Finley held a firm smile and said, "I'll have what Jack is having. Thank you."

"Mmm-hmmm." Maeve swaggered away with both of their eyes following her to the kitchen.

"Care to join me?" Jackson's invitation was easy.

"I'd love to. It's not every day I get to interact with anybody this early. Blair is winning the coffee game so I'm thrust out into the cold to get a good wake-me-up."

"You play a coffee game?"

Finley waved a hand. "Well, she doesn't know we are playing. But I've raced down the last two days to see if I can beat her to the first cup. The whole thing is nearly empty by the time I get to it. She's good, really good."

When Finley looked up after removing her hat, mittens, and jacket, she paused at Jack's amused look. "What?" She laughed, a bit self-consciously.

At first Jackson only shook his head, but couldn't resist the charm in her embarrassment. When she moved a strand of hair that had fallen out of her braid behind her ear, he regretted not moving it for her.

"There might be some fun and excitement left in you yet."

"Left in me?" She laughed. "As if my old age has turned me into a Scrooge."

Jackson let out a deep laugh, but realized he nearly got himself caught. Finley didn't know he was comparing her to the vibrant ten-year-old he once knew, and he wasn't ready for her to know. Not yet, anyway.

"No, it's just very…fitting to the season. Fun and games. Being happy." He shrugged and eyed Finley over his mug of hot chocolate earning a smile.

"Like ordering hot chocolate with marshmallows for breakfast?" she asked.

"Exactly."

Not wanting to interrupt the completely adorable banter her best friend, and what she considered Finley's soul mate, were tossing back and forth, Maeve brought out Finley's order and quietly slipped back to the kitchen where Miles was waiting.

"Well?" he asked.

"He's a Christmas miracle."

They both peeked around the corner of the kitchen and watched a new exchange.

"Hey, it's early, why don't you come up and help me with the first couple cuts of the day?"

The question caught Finley off guard. "I – ah, I should look at my agenda. Is that where you're starting the day?" she asked, flustered at his offer. Which was ridiculous. He was asking her to go work with him, not on a first date.

"Yeah, Blair stole your coffee *and* she caught me on my way over to give me my daily tasks all before breakfast."

"She moves fast." Finley pulled out her phone and opened her calendar, then read it to the both of them. "Wreaths at nine." Her eyes narrowed in confusion. "Santa Claus at three, then…tree lot at six."

"Something wrong?"

"No." Finley looked up. "It's just...empty."

Flicking her finger from left to right to look at the next couple of days and back again, Finley saw they all looked similar. Where was all the running around, checking in with staff? She pulled up the email attachment to her agenda and read:

We are looking great! I'll handle the daily check-ins. Enjoy the day. Supposed to get snow this afternoon. Don't you just love it when it snows on the farm?
Love,
Blair

Well, how do you like that? Finley read it again, bemused.

"Hey, I'm scheduled in the tree lot with you. Looks like Grandpa Chuck's getting a night off. So," he tried again, "what do you say? Trees with me, then I'll help you at the wreath shop?"

Finley nodded once, slowly, then agreed. "Okay, let's do it."

"Great, it's a date! I'll run over and grab the truck while you finish up."

Jack was out the door before Finley could react to anymore of his words. She was going to spend the day with Jack Bloom. He seemed genuinely excited about it. And, it seemed, about spending the day with her.

Interesting.

Finley sipped her hot chocolate and took slow bites of her donut as she watched Jack's shadow walk beneath the floodlights toward the vehicle shed. Her head tilted and she lifted an amused eyebrow as she watched him do a little skip, then disappear behind the farmhouse.

The flutter in her stomach had her taking a breath and pulling her long braid over her shoulder to the front. She massaged her head hoping to add volume to her hair, and followed it with a quick swipe of Chapstick over her lips. She didn't have gloss so she'd have to make do. Then when she went to squint into the window to get a look at her face in the reflection, she caught herself.

What are you doing? she thought.

Quickly straightening in her chair, she flung her braid back and pulled her stocking cap on. "You're working, for goodness sake," she mumbled. "This is *not* a date."

Then suddenly, the years vanished and she was brought back to that day twenty years ago. She remembered the boy, the day, the kiss. Her feelings were a mixture of excitement and guilt. She wanted to be excited, but if she allowed the possibility of something new, did that mean she no longer believed she'd ever see that boy again? That his promise would never be fulfilled?

It was silly, she knew. But a part of her didn't want to let go. What if this was the year he would come back? It made a little part of her close up, to push away her excitement.

"Your chariot awaits," Maeve said, watching the struggle play over her friends' face.

"So, it does." Finley hopped up, maybe a bit too energetically, overcompensating for her childish feelings. "See you later, Maeve."

Maeve watched Jackson beam as Finley jumped into the passenger seat beside him. She noticed Finley's quick laugh at whatever his greeting was, and watched them turn towards the hill. She hoped Finley wouldn't hold back. But hoped more, when it came time for Jackson to tell her who he was, she'd be ready for all the possibilities it held.

"They'll be just fine."

Maeve eyed Miles. "I *know* they will be."

"Then quit hovering, Mother Goose. Come over here, give me a kiss, and help me fill these gingerbread pans."

Maeve walked over, kissed her husband, and took her usual position over rows of bread pans. Turning quietly, she wound a towel around in circles then cracked it like a whip, a bullseye to her husband's bottom. His squeal was more than enough satisfaction.

"You're lucky I love you," she said, before turning her attention back to the gingerbread, knowing there wasn't a more perfect man out there for her than Miles.

"You know," Jack said, as they hauled the chainsaws and axes from the back of the work truck, "I'm getting pretty good at this."

Finley raised a brow as she stretched her muscles, preparing for a morning full of manual labor. "Are you? I did overhear Bobby say you were doing pretty good…for a beginner." She grinned.

"Is that what he said?" Jackson joined in the quick stretch. "I wonder if you'd be willing to test your skills against a *pretty good* beginner?"

Finley tried not to notice his strong body pulling and leaning next to her, and tried not to laugh as Jack grunted out the stretch of a remaining sore and aching muscle. But even with the attractive distractions, she liked her chances.

"It's an interesting challenge. Should we put a wager on it?"

"Now you're talking." Jackson couldn't help but enjoy the game, and was she flirting?

God, he hoped so.

"How about this, the first to ten trees – I'll take this line, you take that one – gets the booth tonight at the lot. The loser," Finley glanced to her left where Jack had taken position next to her, lining up for his row, "is on berry duty at the wreath station and has to haul and tie-down at the lot."

Jackson rubbed his hands together, ready to take on the challenge. There was no way he couldn't win. There wasn't any amount of skill she could have that his physical strength wouldn't beat. He was curious how she'd take the loss. "You. Are. On."

He watched her smile, not even make a motion toward her saw as he counted them down from three to one.

Then, what started as mortification at the rate she was kicking his butt, quickly turned into awe and admiration. He began to laugh heavily at his underestimating her, making it even harder to continue. The only edge it gave him was the harder his laughs came, hers quickly followed.

By the end of the row, Finley had all ten trees lined in a neat row, and she fell to the ground holding her stomach, trying to regain her breath from the work and the breath-stealing laughter. Jackson let himself fall to the ground beside her, laying his whole body flat, exhausted and overjoyed. Silently accepting defeat, and though he had no idea what 'berry duty' meant, he decided it couldn't be that bad especially if it meant spending the day with Finley.

For a moment they just lay side by side, regaining their composure, staring at the sky. Their warm bodies melting what was left of the snow from the fall they'd had a couple days earlier. When Jackson turned to look at Finley, he took in her profile. He watched her eyes close and her lips turn up into a genuine smile. That view was exactly the girl he remembered. Though he didn't know what beauty was when he was younger, then he would have said she was it. But now, her dark lashes, sloping nose, and satisfied mouth - as a man - he knew it to be absolutely true.

"What in Santa's name are you two doing up here?"

Both of their heads lifted off the ground at Bobby's question. Jackson was the first to push himself up, then offered a hand to Finley.

"Getting my butt kicked. Now I'm pouting, like a real man would."

Bobby nodded, understanding completely. "Challenged the farm's best tree cutter, eh?"

Jackson glanced at Finley who tried to look as innocent as possible. "Farm's best tree cutter." Jackson squinted his eyes at her. "Yeah, I guess I did that. And now," Jackson moved toward Bobby and held out a hand for a friendly morning greeting, "I'm on berry and tie-down duty."

"Mm-mm-mm." Bobby shook his head. "I don't envy you. Let me help you load these up and I'll get started on another row. With both of you helping we'll be ahead of schedule today."

"That's the plan. Hence the berries."

"How much time do we have?" Jackson asked the question after they unloaded their last truck full of Christmas trees.

"About a half hour before we should go set up."

"Can I show you something?"

"Do you think there's something on the farm I've not yet seen?"

"There might be something on the farm you haven't seen with me."

Finley stopped and stared at Jack's outstretched hand. The excitement it gave her was both thrilling and moving. When she put her hand in his, she felt his warm fingers wrap around hers, and led her toward the cabins without saying a word.

They continued to walk in silence until they reached the frozen creek behind cabin ten. She let him take her to the edge and finally saw the two chairs at the ice's edge. Looking over, Finley knew he must have brought them down, planning for a moment with her.

They were nestled between leafless winter trees and bushy evergreens, and when she sat, what she saw was spectacular. The blue sky reflected off the frozen pond, and snow that drifted into untidy piles at the edge of the bank. They were only steps from the farm but it was as if they were the only two people for miles.

"It's so peaceful." Finley leaned back in her chair, the picturesque surroundings coaxing her to relax.

"I came out here last night after I went home and packed a few things. I didn't want to stay inside just yet. When I walked down, I couldn't believe the way it looked at night. I figured it couldn't look half bad in daylight either. It was too good not to share."

"Thank you," Finley said, looking at Jack, "for sharing this with me."

"I'm sure you would have found it eventually."

Finley looked out once more. Would she have found it? Would she have taken the time?

"I'm not so sure I would have," she admitted finally. "I used to love this place – every part. And my love was amplified around Christmastime. Spring is beautiful, summer is alive, and fall is like a rusty red, orange, and yellow painting. But winter was enchanting." She glanced over and away again, unable to hold his intense stare, as if he was hanging on every word she said.

"I really thought this place held magic during the winter season. But lately," *nearly two decades,* she thought to herself, "it's slowly lost that magic. But then you showed up – and Nick – and it's like there's new life here. Today, when we were up on the hill, laughing so hard we could barely breathe," she looked down, letting images of her favorite day weave in and out of her mind, "I've felt that way before. That pure joy in the day. I was ten. Can you believe I haven't had a moment like that in twenty years?"

"I've been starting to wonder if everything we do here is worth it. Everything started to feel so mundane. I know I should be grateful, and really, I am. But I was thinking maybe it just wasn't for me anymore," she finished.

"It wouldn't be the same."

Finley looked at Jack, at the seriousness in his eyes.

"How do you know that?"

"I've been here before. A long time ago. It was the best day of my life – one that I've never forgotten. And every day since I've wanted to come back."

It was Jack's turn to look away. He couldn't face the longing in Finley's eyes. He wouldn't be able to hold back his secret if she kept looking at him that way.

"You did that for this place – you *do* that. You make it magical, enchanting. Everything about this place is who you are."

He was worried she'd speak, to try and get more out of him, and he wasn't ready. He loved it here, but he'd yet to settle in, to find his place. So, he forced them to move on. He pulled back his jacket sleeve to look at his watch.

"We should get going. I, for one, don't want to be late for berry duty."

Finley wanted to pry, but she couldn't find the words. Her curiosity yearned to know everything about the day he'd had at the farm, the one he'd never forgotten. But they did have to get to the wreath shop, and as cruel as it was, she was excited to have Jack learn all about berry duty.

Nine hours, a million wreaths, and what seemed like two million Christmas trees later, Jackson sat in the empty bakery staring at his hands.

"What kind of glue *is* that?" he asked, to no one in particular.

Maeve wiped down the counter and the tables around him, and took a second to glance over to see if she could offer any advice.

"Butter."

"Sorry?"

Maeve nodded to Jackson's hands and repeated, "Butter. As much as it pains me to say it knowing that the world's number one baking ingredient could be wasted on glue-hands...butter."

Jackson looked at his hands wondering if that was really all it would take.

"And if that doesn't work; acetone, vegetable oil, warm water, and end with lotion."

Now he smirked. "It's almost like you've been there before."

"My best friend used to be a Christmas nut. I've had more glue on my hands to satisfy me for a lifetime. If she asks me now, I don't even respond. I just turn right around and hide in my kitchen."

"Used to be a Christmas nut?"

Maeve looked up and offered her own sly grin and a nod, then confirmed, "Used to. Though it seems she's found a bit of Christmas cheer the past couple of days. Any idea where that might have come from?"

Jackson wore a proud grin and shrugged. "Not a single clue, unless you have something for me?"

"I like you, Jackson Bloom. And though I might not be the only one, you're not getting more than that out of me."

"Very well." He pushed out of his chair. "Butter." Jackson looked down at his hands then to Maeve who only nodded. "Alright then. See you bright and early."

"Looking forward to it."

CHAPTER 10

The snow had come as the weatherman promised. It started late in the afternoon and fell until well after midnight. It would mean a slow start to the morning, but once the roads cleared, people usually found themselves feeling extra cheerful and wanting to get out to experience the snowy season.

They'd be in for a long, crowded night at the farm. And as Finley sat at her kitchen table, listening to the coffee maker bubbling and gurgling behind her, she realized she wasn't only ready for it, she was excited.

Leaving the full pot of coffee behind, she rushed out into the snow. Her porch had been shoveled, but once she got to the paths leading to the shops, she high-stepped through six inches of beautiful white powder. Laughing with every step, she stomped her boots off once she reached the bakery door, then flung the door open and called for Maeve.

A voice greeted her from the kitchen.

"Who are you, and what have you done with my friend Lee?"

Willing to play along, Finley shouted back, "I'll tell you if you bring me two hot chocolates with marshmallows, two Christmas sprinkle donuts, and two coffees!"

"For here?"

"To go. Please. And thank you!"

Five minutes later, Maeve walked out with a drink carrier and a white paper sack. "I held up my end of the bargain."

"I think the proper question would have been, where did she go, and why is she back?"

Finley snatched the drinks and the bag, then skipped out the door, high-stepping her way across the snow once again. She had a job to do that morning, and she was going to see if she could get a little help.

When Jackson answered the door, he found himself face-to-face with a white bag and paper cups. His eyes gleamed at what he knew sat behind them but didn't want to show it.

She'd never know, but he had watched Finley bound across the snow and into the bakery as he looked out his cabin window. He intended to rush his morning routine, to hurry getting dressed so he could schedule a quick run-in at the bakery, but it looked like he was too slow, and Finley had other plans. Plans that so far, he agreed with.

Jackson took a finger and slowly moved the bag and drinks to the side, finding Finley's face behind them.

"What do I owe the early morning pleasure?" he asked, casually.

"Bribery."

"If that's what I think it is," Jackson said, nodding to the bag and drinks, "so far, it's working. Would you like to come in?"

"I'd love to."

Finley walked in when he took the drinks and moved to the side. She noticed he had already started a fire and wondered if she had finally met a person that woke earlier than she did.

The cabin was so peaceful and comforting to walk into. Finley also noted the newspaper opened to the business pages and folded in half, sitting on the table that centered the two chairs positioned in front of the fire. Beneath the paper, she saw a thriller novel but couldn't describe it beyond recognizing the authors' name and knowing what kind of books he wrote. But something about knowing that's what Jackson did at night or early in the morning felt comforting to her.

"Want to sit by the fire?"

"If you didn't offer, I would have asked."

Jackson held a guiding hand out toward one of the high-back leather chairs, meant for lounging in the evening, and Finley followed when she removed her boots. She took in the spacious cabin and the Christmas decorations that had been added just before Thanksgiving in anticipation of the new occupants.

A soaring, fresh balsam fir stretched over ten feet in the two-story living room. Different sizes of twinkling white lights wrapped endlessly around its body. And bronze, gold, and wooden bulbs and ornaments draped nearly every sturdy limb. The stair banisters and the fireplace mantle were wrapped in garland. And where scenic pictures and simple décor had been minimally placed throughout the living area, wintery Christmas scenes and rustic winter statues and little trees had taken their place. Though she couldn't see them, the bedrooms had all been transformed and turned down with plush, forest green comforters with fluffy pillows and throws.

Finley knew every detail of each cabin, as she'd been the one to design and decorate them. They were intended to be used all year long, but every decision she'd made had Christmas in mind.

Tucking her feet beneath her, Finley hugged her coffee, closed her eyes, and breathed in comfort.

"I love these cabins." She opened her eyes to see Jack looking at her like he could sit and look and listen to her for hours. It softened and stirred something inside of her simultaneously. Not knowing how to react, she continued. "My dad did the work on the farm, but my mom, these were her babies. And it was so fun getting to work with her on them. It was the last project we took on together before they retired."

"Where are they now?"

"Basking in the Carolina sunshine," Finley answered, then took a sip of the decadent brown liquid in her cup.

"I see the appeal of retirement. But after being here for a couple of days, I'm not sure I wouldn't miss the winter," Jackson admitted, knowing just a week ago he would have hopped a plane to any state regardless of the weather if it meant he could retire. Now, he'd seriously consider retiring to a farm – this one in particular, if they'd have him.

"What do you do?"

Jackson looked at Finley with a charming grin. "I don't come off as a tradesman to you?"

"I know a slick corporate man when I see one." Finley let a playful smile twitch her lip. "Your wool jacket and high-end department store suit gave you away when we met. But," she continued, "you pass as a decent tradesman."

"I'll take a compliment where I can get one." Jackson mirrored Finley's sip of coffee and leaned toward the bag of donuts before continuing; he offered Finley the first pick before reaching in for his own.

"I work with my dad and brothers – two of them, Jake and James. We have an outdoor recreation retail chain, mostly in the Midwest and Northeast areas. It started with a love of the outdoors – probably why I love working here so much – but somehow ended up with the four of us locked in an office building twelve hours a day, five days a week."

"Retail? Isn't this kind of a busy time for you? Are you sure you should be working *here?*" Finley hid the worry in her question. She didn't want Jack to leave but hoped their conversation didn't put unnecessary pressure on him if he was teetering on the fence of coming or going.

"Let's just say my brother, Jake, isn't overly excited about my timing. But I told him I would make some progress on a project while I was out." Jackson lifted his mug, toasting to himself and his terrible idea. "I'll start working on that sometime in the next couple of days."

His nonchalant attitude reassured her that he wouldn't leave if he could help it, but she couldn't help but wonder if this project of his wasn't getting the attention it needed. He didn't seem interested in getting on with it, which she supposed wasn't her business as long as the job he did on the farm lived up to her high standards.

And this year, more than any before, she understood the desire to escape. Hadn't she, only a couple days ago, confided in Maeve about wanting something similar? And not just a break, but tossing around the idea of not working the farm at all.

Finley nodded her understanding. "Well, we'll take you as long as we can have you. You're a breath of fresh air, and everybody has loved having you around. And," she didn't know what compelled her to continue, "if you ever want to talk about it, I feel like we might have enough in common in that area to have a nice conversation about it."

Jackson wanted to ask, *everybody has loved? Or you have?*

He wished that was her feeling more than anything. But after just a couple of days, how could he really expect those feelings from a woman who didn't really know who he was? Who had probably forgotten that day so long ago?

Instead, for now, he just nodded. And seeing as he didn't leave a crumb of his Christmas donut behind, he figured he could segue.

"So, you said you were bribing me. Seeing as I just polished off the bribe, what's the task?"

"How do you feel about shoveling?"

While they worked, Jackson and Finley stole secret glances at each other. Neither willing to let the other see they were watching, but feeling hopeful the other was thinking about them.

Finley admitted to herself there was an ease, a comfort, of being with Jack. It settled her more than she expected, but that didn't make it any less unnerving.

He seemed a magnet for fun – an enthusiast for appreciation. More than once, when she looked over, she caught him smiling at the simplest task: completing a final row of shoveling off the cabin porch or glancing at the hazy glow of a lamp. When he'd dumped a pile of snow from his porch to hers, he laughed like crazy as she ran over to it, trying to heave it back to his side.

Then, when they'd finished shoveling and were out of breath, he'd walked over to where she was standing on the final porch and offered his hand to help her down.

Finley noticed their puffs of breath cloud the cold air in front of them and grabbed his hand to let him help her down. It was then when she wondered what it would be like to hold his hand for no reason at all, just for the simple purpose of wanting to touch him.

The thought caused her hand to pull away too quickly when she reached the pavement, but she felt the warmth linger. It was a comfort she'd felt only once before, but this time it was more than a long-ago memory. It felt real and vivid. Without reason, it caused a little burn on her cheek where a boy had placed a kiss before he walked out of her life forever.

Katie Bachand

CHAPTER 11

It was four-thirty in the morning, and Finley was staring out of her bedroom window. She was watching a light dusting of snowfall outside, illuminated by the farm floodlights that lit the grounds at night. Her alarm clock would have forced her out of bed at five, but when she woke, the idea of another day had her stretching and lifting the covers off.

Rather than rush, she pulled the crimson throw placed at the edge of her bed around her winter flannel pajamas and took in the view. Every once in a while, she let her eyes drift toward cabin number ten and wondered if Jack was awake, taking in a slow morning like she was. Or if his alarm clock would wake him up, and he'd be in a rush to get out the door.

After a while, seeing no signs of life, she wandered to her closet. Holding the blanket in place with one hand, she shuffled through her shirts with the other. Filing through, one by one, passing all of the checkered, polka dot, and solid-colored button shirts, Finley found a bright red sweater she'd not worn in what could possibly be years.

Tossing it and a pair of jeans on the bed, she turned to her dresser. For the first time in a long time took care to put on mascara and a bit of blush. A wistful memory caused a slow smile to form on her face. She remembered a time when she'd had to sneak the action, and because of it, just for a bit of fun, she added gloss to her lips.

Because she couldn't quite think of anything else to do with her hair that wouldn't be ruined in seconds by her cap and the weather, she braided the thick strands like she did every day, then dressed for the day ahead.

Without turning toward the kitchen, Finley pulled on her winter gear before taking her first steps out the door. Her walk was slow across to the shops, letting cold take away the heat she'd built up inside.

For the first time in a long time, she was energized for the day. As her boots crackled on the gravel road, she felt a twinge of hope she'd see Jack inside the bakery when she walked in.

Wasn't that an interesting feeling? She wondered as she pulled the door open if he might feel the same about her.

The bakery was empty in the customer area, but Finley could hear the clattering of heavy metal pans, dishes crashing into the industrial sink, and the faint voices of Maeve and Miles talking together and singing to the Christmas music they played all season long.

Rather than ruin the moment by yelling back to them, she reached around the counter for a mug and filled it to the brim with coffee.

Filling her cup and inhaling the rich scent, she thought about the light crowd they'd have that morning – the first weekday after the Thanksgiving holiday. Most people would be headed back to work, putting in their time so they could take those few precious days off around Christmas.

She imagined they felt much like she did, that the days seemed a little more cheerful and a little easier to get through in the weeks leading up to the holiday. Something about knowing Christmas would soon be there. The prepping, the presents, the baking, the food. All of it would consume a happy part of people's minds as they worked, leaving what she thought was a little less room for deadlines and worry.

When Finley sat, she pulled out her phone to see where Blair had placed her that day. Scrolling through her messages, then once more to double-check, she realized the agenda hadn't yet been sent.

"That's interesting," Finley said aloud to herself, just as the door swung open.

Like a blizzard disrupting the calm winter morning, Blair rushed in.

"Hi! Oh good, you're here!" Blair pulled off her jacket and sat down across from Finley. Then immediately shot back up, mirroring

Finley's previous reach for a mug from behind the counter to fill her own steaming cup, talking the whole while she moved.

"I was up most of the night putting a couple ideas together to show you – I'm totally excited about them. But I fell asleep at my desk – grandma's desk. Still weird to call it mine."

Finley only grinned at the mile-a-minute young woman and the idea that her grandmothers' desk was getting good use since Blair claimed the room. Something about the vacant space being filled made it feel more like home.

"Anyway," Blair continued, "I forgot to set my alarm, thinking I'd set it a bit earlier than normal to finish a few things up, and wouldn't you know it, pretty soon I'm drooling on my papers, and it's already five o'clock. I didn't even have time to make coffee. And that's why you don't have your agenda." Blair sat and nodded to the phone that still sat in Finley's hand where she was studying it before.

"I think we'll manage if the schedule is one hour early rather than three." Finley leaned back and grinned.

"Ha-ha, very–whoa." Blair held up short from delivering a sarcastic comment, finally taking the time to pause and look at Finley. "Look at you. What's the occasion?"

"I'm wearing a sweater. I wear sweaters."

"Maybe twice a year. And you're wearing makeup. Ohh."

The *Ohh* was dragged out just long enough for Finley to roll her eyes, but she couldn't keep the flutter and the quick youthful smile from coming.

"Oh my *god*. It's *the guy*. It's Jack, isn't it?"

Unwilling to admit she'd begun to get giddy at the idea of seeing him, she didn't want to let her cousin down.

"Come on, like you don't think he's cute?"

"Cute?" Blair's eyebrows furrowed together in a perfected show of attitude. "I think you mean dreamy. He's totally handsome. Cute is for college dudes. Or, like, that guy that plays Spider Man."

Finley couldn't hold back the laugh. Blair had a point, though she couldn't quite pin-point Spider Man.

"Okay, he's handsome. I'll give you that."

"And funny. And smart. And totally works hard."

Finding what was left of her younger self, Finley said, "Well, why don't you chase him down then?"

"What? Yuck," Blair's face pinched together, "He's *so* old."

"Excuse me?"

"I mean – whatever, you know what I mean."

"Oh, do I?"

"You're not old. You're just more Jack's age. Primed for the kind of relationship that lasts longer than three months."

"Is that right?" Finley tried for humor. "So, you're telling me you'd shoot down Brad Pitt or George Clooney?"

Blair's lips pinched together, and she said nothing.

"Ha! My point exactly."

"What are you two yelling about out here? And why didn't either of you call back to the kitchen? We have fresh cranberry bread and gingerbread muffins."

Maeve set a sample of both on the table between the women.

"Blair just called me old."

"I did not!"

"Lee," Maeve said, "we *are* old."

"Thirty is not old."

"Did you *really* think we would *ever* be this age?" Maeve pressed.

Finley sipped, remembering the past two decades, how she'd pleaded for the days – the years – to go by, but not wanting to age. Unable to fathom that one day she'd no longer be a kid.

"No," she admitted, "and I sure as heck didn't think I'd be alone."

"Well, go hitch yourself to Jack. He seems ripe for the taking."

"You, too?" Finley asked.

"That *is* why you have makeup and a cute little sweater on today, isn't it?"

Finley stared after Maeve, who left without giving her a chance to respond, then looked over to see Blair giving her the *I told you* stare.

"Yeah, yeah," was all she said before changing the subject. "Let's see today's agenda."

Jack stood for a long time outside of the bakery watching the three women exchange words and bouts of laughter. He could tell from their animated body language and amused facial expressions they were engulfed in each other and the conversation. It was too good of a moment to break up. But when he watched Maeve sashay back to the kitchen, he saw his opening.

By the time he drew the door open, Finley and Blair were head-down over one of their phones. Both heads turned at the sound he made walking in.

Jackson noticed Blair beam, and Finley offered a casual smile and a hint of blush on her cheeks. Immediately he wished he could have been a fly on the wall for their previous conversation. Jackson also noticed the bright red of Finley's sweater bringing out her deep brown eyes and the cheeks she'd taken care to add a bit of flush to that day. He wasn't stuck up enough to assume it was for him, but he was humble enough to hope.

Just when he thought she couldn't have done anything more to make him fall for her all over again, a simple, innocent look took his breath away.

"Just the man *we* were hoping to see this morning," Blair started as he walked toward their table.

Jackson didn't miss the squint Finley shot Blair at her use and emphasis on *'we.'*

"Is that right?" he asked, hoping he sounded innocent enough.

"It is. How do you feel about baking?"

Eyes wide and movements stopped, Jackson looked from one woman to the other. "About the same as I feel about getting a tetanus shot or stubbing my toe. Why?"

"Perfect! You can help Finley in the kitchen this afternoon while Maeve and Miles are out."

"Ah," Jackson's face looked as confused as he felt, "I'm not sure my response was received as I intended it to be. I don't think you want me in the kitchen – around anything that somebody else might want to enjoy." Jackson pondered his words. "Unless it's exclusive to taste-testing."

Finley sat back, excited to see how Blair would kindly tell him he didn't have a choice. She also realized this was something that might have irritated her before, but knowing that Jack was going to get a taste of the hard time she'd received earlier felt a little nice.

Blair began, "It's baking. You can hardly screw it up. Follow the recipes exactly, bake for the right amount of time, and there you have it. You'll be an expert in no time. Besides, Finley can help you. If anything doesn't turn out, just blame her. She's the owner, remember? Nothing is really ever your fault."

"Wait," Finley said, after a few seconds, realizing what Blair had said, "is that how you operate?"

"For sure." Blair beamed, satisfied with herself and her humor. "I'm only as good as you let me be."

When Finley looked to Jack for support, she realized she was outnumbered. His goofy grin matched her cousin's.

"So, Jack, what do you say? Kitchen duty?" Blair smirked.

"You know, I think I might be changing my tune. Kitchen duty sounds like it might be right up my alley."

"Great! Then, I'll leave you two to it. Maeve and Miles will give you the run-down before they head out. See you later!"

Finley waited until Blair was out the door before she darted her eyes toward Jack.

"What?" Jack feigned innocence.

"Stubbing your toe?"

"I mean, how bad can it be, really?"

Finley had been there before; she'd had the *run-down*. But when she slid an eye toward Jack in the middle of their bakery operations crash-course, she saw a deer in headlights. Stunned and unable to move. She wondered how much he was actually taking in at this point.

"All of the soups are made," Miles continued with his lunch and dinner lecture, "croissants and sandwiches are premade and stored. All you have to do is take them out of the right container and pop them in the oven for the specified amount of time. Cheat-sheets are hanging above the dressing station.

"Around one-thirty, you'll have a lull; that's when you start with the second round of Christmas cookies. Today we are scheduled for gingerbread, chocolate crinkles, dipped shortbread, cranberry biscotti, and almond pretzel sticks. Maeve pre-sorted the ingredients for you; all you have to do is follow the recipe, measure, bake, and decorate. She's learned over the years to snap a picture of the final product so you'll know exactly what everything should look like. Straight-forward." Miles's hand sliced the air as if he was giving driving directions. "Any questions?"

Jack finally blinked a couple times and moved his head from Miles to Finley and back again.

"Yes."

Miles nodded, then waited. When nothing happened, he encouraged, "Yes, you have questions?"

"Yes."

"Alright, shoot."

"I don't know what they are right now, but I know I have questions."

Laughing, Miles slapped a hand on Jack's shoulder and let it rest there. "Don't worry, you'll get the hang of it. And just remember. One customer at a time, be friendly, and the best part is: everybody that comes here is happy because it's like a Christmas playground."

Jackson let his head bob up and down, then he walked away, head down, reading the list Maeve had written out.

"Everybody's happy?" Finley smiled at Miles, imagining the over-tired kids, the overachieving parents, and the endless line for Santa Claus that made for testing everybody's limits.

"He looked like he needed a little encouragement."

"That was nice of you," Finley said as Miles turned to look at Maeve, who always got a little quiet on appointment days. She asked gently, "How are you two doing?"

Miles did his best to show good spirits and said, "We make it through just fine. And I'll be darned if no matter how bad it is while we're in there, we love each other more when we walk out again."

"There isn't a greater love in the world. I'll give you that. Be strong. And know I love you both so much," Finley said, her heart aching for her friends.

"It's what gets us through. You got everything under control?"

"For you and Maeve, we'd conquer just about anything you could throw at us. We'll see you tonight. And as usual, let me know if you don't feel like heading back."

"You know we will. But what better place to be when you need a little pick-me-up?"

Miles winked, headed in Maeve's direction, and within five minutes, they were out the door. She and Jack were officially on their own. Actually, at the present moment, *she* was alone. Well, she figured Jack would be back as soon as he came to grips with his latest assignment.

"Might as well get started." Finley tied on their farm's signature dark green apron, slid on some kitchen gloves, and pulled up the list.

"Caramel rolls," she said aloud, "easy-peasy."

Twenty minutes in, Finley had the dough rolled out along a big stainless island in the kitchen when she realized she hadn't heard the chime of a bell letting her know a customer was waiting, and she had yet to see Jack walk back in.

Finley generously buttered the thick layer of dough, heavy-handed the cinnamon, sugar, and nutmeg mixture, then sprinkled a few pecans on the top before she rolled the dough into a long, spiraling log.

Perfection, she thought. Then curiosity got the best of her.

When she moved out of the kitchen, away from the whirring mixers, humming ovens, and simmering sauces, she realized it hadn't been as quiet as she thought – and she definitely wasn't the only one working. When she poked her head around the corner, she saw Jack moving efficiently from register to fridge, to coffee canisters, and back again. All with a trying smile plastered on his face. The sight nearly made her laugh, but she covered her mouth with a buttery, sugar-covered glove to stifle her amusement and kept watching.

It was amazing. His movements were robotic, his interactions on auto-pilot. Every action down to the detail of what Miles said, and the written instructions had described: take money, heat food, prepare the to-go container, say *'thank you,'* smile, repeat.

Finley thought about helping him but couldn't get herself to break his concentrated rhythm. Besides, the line wasn't unmanageable quite yet, and the lunch crowd was a couple hours off. She might as well keep going with the baking so they'd have something to serve.

The monotony of slicing the cinnamon rolls with a string and placing them in their pans allowed her mind to wander. She thought about Maeve and Miles and sent up a silent prayer their appointment was going well. She wondered what her parents were doing on the eastern shoreline. And she smiled when her mind settled on Jack. He'd found a way to bring her back. Sure, she was the one that had to *enjoy,* but she wondered just how much enjoyment she'd really be having had he not shown up with Nick.

A small part of her wondered – no, hoped – Jack was more than a passing stranger. She felt pulled to him in a way she couldn't explain. Where others before him – though there weren't many, there were some – had only made her wish for the feeling she'd had when she was ten, here was Jack, filling those needs. Where Finley once felt the guilt of moving on, the fear of letting the long-ago promise slip away, there was now hope that Jack could fill that void. And perhaps more than a void, maybe he could be her happily ever after.

"Wow." The thought caused Finley to stop her work and look up, wondering if she meant it.

Happy ever after.

Really?

"Couldn't be," she finally said aloud.

Her shocked face turned to the two-way door when it pushed open, Jack moved into the threshold. He had one hand on the door and the other on the frame, as if he was single-handedly holding the building in place.

"I am an order-taking, breakfast-making, customer-thanking aficionado. I should be the poster-child for bakeries everywhere."

"Yes," Finley agreed, giggling, "yes, you are. And yes, you should be."

The kitchen looked as if a pack of toddlers and puppies had been let loose to play. Every inch of the counter, and most of the floor, was covered in flour. Sticky white goop was found wherever flour had mixed with spilled eggs, milk, vanilla, or any other wet ingredient that had flung out of a mixer or bowl.

When Finley looked up from dropping big chocolate dough balls for the crinkles on a sheet pan, she saw flour had even dusted the top of Jack's head. The sight caused a snort as she tried to stifle a laugh that caught Jack's attention.

"What?" he asked while meticulously dipping shortbread cookies into melted chocolate, then dipping them into a bowl of chopped pistachios.

"Oh, nothing." Finley lifted the corner of her lip while shaking her head as if nothing had caught her attention.

"No, no. I'm *baking*. I have turned myself into a bakery and cookie master. I deserve to know what you find so amusing." He pointed a dripping chocolate-coated spoon in Finley's direction, flinging a droplet across the table onto her sweater sleeve.

When Jack saw what he did, his eyes grew wide in playful fear.

"Ohh," Finley said through bubbling laughter, "you just flung chocolate at me."

Jack set the spoon down and lifted his hands in the air, trying to prove innocence. He slowly started to move around the island in Finley's direction, picking up a wet dishcloth on the way.

"Hold on, hold on. I'm coming to make peace." Jackson tentatively made the final step closing the gap between them. "I'm just going to…"

He lifted her hand to move her arm closer to him, then gently wiped the chocolate off her sleeve. When he finished, he looked up and noticed the way she was looking at him had changed. The goofy grin was gone, the curve in her lip had settled, and her eyes searched.

Finley wondered if he noticed when he took her hand, her pulse quickened. When he looked up, was he able to tell she was speechless? Did he know she yearned to know what he was thinking right at that moment, or that something inside of her wished he would kiss her?

Rather than answer her silent questions aloud, he lifted his hand to her cheek and slowly began wiping away the flour she hadn't realized dusted her own face. Then, as if magic itself was the cause, he leaned his face into hers.

"Hey! We are out of Gingerbread cookies!" Blair shouted her way through the door. She stopped short from coming all the way in when she saw what she was about to interrupt. "Oh! *Ohh,* I'll just–" she pointed back toward the front of the shop and hurried out.

The moment ended as they both bashfully looked away. But the innocent way they jumped apart, as if they were school-aged kids getting caught with the door closed, had them both smiling.

"I should," Jack started, nodding to the finished sheet of gingerbread men, "you know, bring these out."

Finley nodded her agreement and watched as he paused just before walking through the swinging door.

"What if I asked you to spend the evening with me tomorrow? After work, I mean."

Finley felt the burn of blush on her cheeks as she wrapped her arms around her waist. It did little to settle her nerves, but every flutter was worth it as it's what she wanted most aside from their missed kiss.

"I'd love that."

"Good, me too."

Then Jack moved through the door to drop off their first successful batch of cookies.

CHAPTER 12

The new day started early, just like the one before it. There wasn't snow or sunshine, only a gray overcast sky, chilly winds, and slushy paths. The gray days usually meant more clean-up work, more sanding and salting streets and entryways, sweeping and mopping at the end of the day, and extra Christmas cheer to beat the gloom.

Usually.

But as Finley moved through her day, all she could think about was her date with Jack that evening, and gloom was nowhere in sight. They had settled on seven. Finley would finish helping at Santa's workshop and make sure the outdoor movie scheduled for eight was ready to go, then she'd be free. And Blair, not so surprisingly, was more than happy to shuffle some schedules around to give them the free night, especially after the sight they made in the kitchen the day before.

Even the thought of her cousin bouncing on her bed the night before, 'ooh-ing and ahh-ing' at the winter night date, caused more excitement rather than nerves. Though, she had plenty of those too.

Finley didn't quite know how she made it through the morning, but somehow the afternoon was upon her. Now, as she wandered through Santa's workshop, she added decorative presents, fresh red and white Poinsettias, and organized little stands that lured families to the Christmas shop, she realized her date with Jack was drawing near.

Date? Finley took the time to consider the term and deemed it appropriate after their almost-kiss.

Humming a bit to the Christmas music that drifted throughout the farm and through the workshop speakers, she let herself get lost in the small details of the job. Before long, she heard rustling from the back of the shop and a door open and close, bringing with it a swift cold breeze.

"Well, doesn't this look just wonderful!"

Finley came around the corner to see Nick circling the room in appreciation for what she'd done.

"Thanks. I agree. It doesn't look too bad."

"Too bad?" Nick questioned. "It looks nearly as good as Mrs. Cla–" Nick hesitated for only a bit, deciding it couldn't hurt to hold character while he was there, "Claus' decorating at home."

Finley gave him a goofy grin and nodded, wondering if his wife enjoyed being referred to as 'Mrs. Claus.' If she was anything like Nick, she supposed it was a welcomed reference.

"I don't want to speak out of turn..." Nick began, as he removed his thick brown jacket to start his wardrobe change, and brought Finley out of her thought.

"Something I can't imagine you doing." Finley smiled. "By all means, continue."

"I can't help but see a bit of a change in you. You seem *filled.*" Nick nodded at his choice of words, even with Finley's questioning stare.

"Filled?" she asked.

"Yes. With spirit. Filled with happiness. And," Nick moved closer to her, "if I look just close enough, dare I say it, love."

Finley took in the rosy cheeks and the bright eyes of the man standing before her, lost in his suggestion and the enchantment that seemed to surround him as he spoke.

"Love?" This time she heard and questioned only the latter, seeing as she was filled. More than she'd been in a long time.

"

Oh, yes. I'm a great spotter of love. It's what I love most, after all. In my line of work, I sometimes have to look a little deeper than actions, than what's on the surface. I've gotten very good at seeing the love that lies beneath. Though yours seems to radiate. It's quite splendid."

Rather than argue or press, Finley accepted the assessment. Love might be a stretch, but whatever she was feeling was spectacular, and she didn't want it to end.

As Santa slipped away to change into his jolly red suit, and Finley started to get back to her tasks, Maeve rushed in.

"Maeve?" Finley looked up, worried at her panting friend. "Are you okay?"

"Only have ten minutes. Tried calling. Not answering." Maeve pointed to Finley, a small accusation.

Finley patted her pockets. "Huh, I must have left my phone in the office this morning, sorry." She walked to Maeve taking her hand. "What can I do? Let me help."

"No help, just talk. Do you have ten minutes?"

"You have all afternoon!" Both women turned to the changing room, where Nick's cheerful voice stretched over to them.

"How in the world did he hear that?" Finley asked, looking at Maeve, who was equally impressed but unable to express it with words as her breathing was coming back but still escaping her.

"Thanks, Nick – will be back shortly."

"No rush whatsoever!"

Maeve led Finley through the outdoor slush and into the bakery, ignoring Finley's barrage of questions. They moved through the kitchen and lifted their noses to inhale the freshly frosted sugar cookies, then rushed into the small office carved into the back corner of the space. Maeve took Finley's hand and placed her in one chair while she took the other.

Even before she started to speak, Maeve's eyes filled with tears.

And though she tried to hold them back, fearing the worst, Finley covered her mouth with her hand as a quick gasp caught her breath and tears filled her own eyes. She slowly shook her head, not wanting to hear what Maeve was about to tell her. Learning her friend had been diagnosed with cancer the first time was hard enough. She didn't know if she could hear it again.

"No," Maeve whispered, "not like that."

Finley wiped at tears and a running nose. "I don't understand."

"It's been five years," Maeve said smiling, "and it hasn't come back. And," Maeve squeezed the hand she held, "at our last visit three months ago, we were approved to start fertility treatments. So..."

"Oh, my God." It started as a whisper. Finley repeated it with more excitement than she'd ever said anything. "Oh, *my God!*"

Maeve only nodded. Then, with both women crying happy tears, she said, "We are going to have a baby!"

Christmas was the season for miracles. Finley floated through the next hour, happier than she'd ever been. Her heart swelled. It was nearly bursting as she went around greeting customers, playing with the kids who cared just as little about the cloudy day as she did.

After a cup of mid-afternoon hot chocolate, she decided it was about time to head to her office and get some paperwork done. As much as she wished the farm would run itself, there were numbers to crunch, profits to analyze, employees – who were more like family – to pay.

Finley made a quick stop in the farmhouse living room. She made sure the Christmas tree lights were on, lit some of the cinnamon-cider candles placed throughout the room, and put her grandpa's old record player on. It wouldn't be as convenient as listening to the radio that boasted Christmas music throughout the day as the holidays came and went. Still, there was something earthy and heartwarming about the crackles and fuzz that sang along with Bing Crosby and Rosemary Clooney.

After losing herself in an hour of work, Finley stretched, checked the clock, and saw it was already five-thirty. She could afford to take a little break to go set up the movie for tonight's showing, then hop back inside to freshen up before her date with Jack.

"My date with Jack," Finley said to herself, liking the way it sounded, as she passed the Christmas tree lot and waved to Grandpa Chuck. When he blew her a kiss, she caught it on a laugh, thinking something so sweet was all the sweeter when it came from a rugged old man whose hands had seen more hard labor in their lives than most. Especially when they wore thick yellow work gloves that had dirtied over the years, and his white hair looked a little like it had gone through the gust of a snowy whirlwind.

When Finley reached the open field with strategically placed hay bales that stretched hundreds of feet up a slow slant so any who sat could have a good view of the outdoor movie screen, she hopped over a couple bales until she reached the middle. There sat a little wooden box kept warm with the help of a small generator where the projector would play tonight's feature film. She reached for her phone and realized she'd left it at the house again.

Hmm, she thought. First Tuesday of the season. Had to be *The Grinch.* And if not, it wouldn't take long to swap out at the last minute. So, she fired up the projector to get it warm, then hit play to make sure there wouldn't be any hiccups. Clicking back to the menu, but leaving the projector on, her job was done. Blair would make sure the movie played on schedule – as usual.

"As usual," Finley said to herself, thinking about Blair and how much she'd taken on this year. On the thought, she made a mental note to look at her calendar and put something on Blair's agenda for a change. She'd make an effort to book time with Blair so she could tell her all about her new ideas she'd been dreaming up. What better way to repay somebody who has done so much for you?

"Finley?"

Finley turned to see Blair calling her name and waving her arms to get her attention. Finley waved back, showing she'd heard, and pushed off the ground to make her way back.

"Hey, Finley."

"Yeah, what's up, Blair?"

"I got a call from a guy who's coming by to see you." Blair grinned. "Said he's been calling you all day but hasn't been able to reach you."

"Makes sense."

"Huh?" Blair wondered, looking perplexed.

"I haven't had my phone on me all day. Forgot it in the house. You said he's coming by?"

"Yeah, he said six o'clock."

"Did he tell you what he wanted?"

"Not even a little bit. Just asked for you specifically. I went in to pour you both some hot chocolate and turn on some tunes. I flipped the record. You beat me to that idea today."

"I did. Okay, I'll head back in now. You're sure you've got everything handled for tonight?"

Blair only smiled devilishly, as a young woman who knew what kind of a good night Finley had ahead of her.

"Okay, yeah, I see you'll be just fine. Gimme a break." Finley rolled her eyes and laughed.

"Oh, I will give you all the breaks you need if it means you'll be spending more time with *Jack.*"

Pointing a finger in Blair's direction, Finley jokingly reprimanded, "You, Miss, know far too much. Go mind your business and let me have a perfect winter night's date."

"Done, and done." Blair turned to move toward the shops but paused after only a step. "Hey, Lee?"

"Yeah?"

"You know I love you, right?"

Finley nodded. "Not as much as I love you."

When Finley walked into her office she had to hide a grin and compose herself. The man had beaten her to the office, but his city-slicker attire is what egged her amusement on. She walked the rest of the way in, taking him in as she offered a greeting.

He was a bit shorter than she was and slightly rounded at the waist. But she noted his graying hair was slicked back and stuck to his head with what must have been shiny glue as it didn't move an inch as he turned. His suit fit him as if it had been sewn on him while he wore it, and his shoes, though he walked through pathways of muck and snow to get to her office, were already wiped and polished. She wondered how he'd done that so quickly, and if it was worth the effort knowing he'd be back outside within the hour and she'd be well on her way to Jack's.

"Good evening, sir. Can I help you?"

"Finley Whittaker, I presume?"

Finley nodded. "With whom do I have the pleasure?" She held out her hand as she settled herself behind her desk. They shook and she held a gesturing hand to the chair across from hers so he could sit.

"My name is Connor Jorgenson. I own and operate the Jorgenson Group out of St. Paul."

Finley only nodded, not having heard of the group, and waited for Mr. Jorgenson to continue.

Only a little put off that his name wasn't recognized, Connor continued. "I don't want to be rude or frank, and I apologize for just stopping by, but I tried to call all day and couldn't get through."

"Yes, my apologies, I didn't have my phone with me today. I'm glad you came in and caught me. What can I do for you?" Finley prompted, hoping he'd get on with it but not wanting to be rude.

"Right. If I'm cutting right to the chase, I hope you understand I don't intend to be rude. I'm simply sharing my intentions."

Finley nodded her appreciation.

"I'd like to buy Winter Haven."

"Oh." Finley didn't know what to say, as that was the last thing she anticipated hearing. She imagined somebody wanting to buy a large portion of their tree crop or wanting a corporate discount, but not the entire farm.

"Ah, yes, well."

"Yes?" Connor questioned, wondering if she'd said 'yes' to his request.

"Oh, no. Or, sorry, Mr. Jorgenson, I apologize. I wasn't prepared for that to be the request. That's something that would take serious consideration. We'd need to have more than a five-minute conversation, not including introductions."

Her guest smiled and said, "That's what I assumed, but hoped for the best." He took a long breath and she waited for him to continue. "You have beautiful land. I'm guessing Doug Fir on the hills for good drainage, Pine just about everywhere else. Good ground accessibility throughout your acreage – well-kept roads. Buildings on the grounds are beautiful and impeccably maintained. You've already started a row of cabins."

Interesting, Finley thought of his choice of words, 'already started a row of cabins,' meaning he was interested in more?

"You've just expanded to over one-hundred acres, or that's what I could find in my initial research."

Connor hoped to get a verbal or non-verbal indication he was right but was met with nothing but Finley's attention. "So, I understand a fair market price for the land alone – if we were calculating at one-hundred acres – would be just over one million. Your cabins add between two-fifty and three apiece. Then there's the farmhouse," Connor paused and looked around, pleased, "that is in immaculate condition – probably seven to eight-hundred even in this small town. And the shops. All outfitted, and one with a full restaurant kitchen. I'd say that's at least another five."

Connor Jorgenson shifted in his chair, moving forward to rest his elbows on the edge of Finley's desk. "If my math serves me–"

"Five-point-three." Finley calculated his numbers for him and solemnly took in his appreciative look.

"Yes," he confirmed, "and I'm willing to offer you seven - not including a detailed business discussion I'm assuming we would need to have. I'm very interested in this property. I'm not ashamed to say I took the liberty of enjoying it today for a bit once I got here."

"Well, thank you for saying that. A lot of hard work, over many years, has turned it into what it is today."

Finley sat in silence for a moment. She wished she had time to weigh the pros and cons. To assess how she felt about the farm now that she was enjoying herself. She wondered what Blair and Maeve would have to say about it, or her parents. She wished she could talk about it with Jack, to have an unbiased opinion – though he seemed to love the farm, so it might not be as impartial as she'd like. But as she looked at the clock and saw it was nearly time for her to go to Jack's, Finley knew the time to rush to a decision wasn't today – or probably even tomorrow. She would think about it, about how to include the others, then decide.

"I don't want to rush your decision," Connor said, interrupting Finley's thoughts, "but this is something I'd like to move on quickly if you're seriously interested."

"What's your deadline?" Finley asked, curious as to why the rush, but the reason itself shouldn't impact her decision.

"I'd like to have an answer by Christmas. I have a big year ahead, and I'd like to know what I'm moving forward with."

"Understood." Finley stood, not wanting to rush Mr. Jorgenson out, but she wanted her own space for a moment. "I apologize for the abrupt ending to our meeting, Mr. Jorgenson, but I'm afraid I have another engagement I have to get to. Is there a way I can contact you?"

Readier for their meeting than she realized, Finley watched as her guest pulled a large file out of his briefcase along with a business card that had his name and his company in bold letters across the front.

"This is how I came up with our initial offer." Connor pointed to the file folder. "And this is my card." He handed both to Finley.

"Thank you."

"You can get a hold of me any time, day or night, for your decision. Again, I'm very interested."

Finley held out her free hand for a second time, watched him shake it, and said, "Thank you, this is something we won't take lightly, I assure you. Can I walk you out?"

"Oh, I think I'll be able to find my way. I might head across the way and make a pitstop at that bakery of yours on my way out. Thank you for your time."

On a nod, Finley watched Mr. Jorgenson wrap a scarf around his neck and place a top-hat on his head, then head across to the shops. When she couldn't see him through the window anymore, she fell back into her chair. Deciding not to flip the file open, she just sat and closed her eyes.

Seven million dollars.

She repeated the number in her head a few times before sliding the folder to the side of her desk and placing the business card inside.

Finley took a moment to laugh and wonder where this guy was a week ago when she'd felt lost and overworked? She wondered how quickly she would have jumped at the chance to sell even days ago.

But now? After the fun, after genuinely participating in and appreciating the farm, after Jack...

"Crap! Jack!"

Finley looked at the clock once more and realized she was late. She pushed herself up and took ten seconds to make a quick decision: be late and run upstairs to freshen up, check her clothes, update her makeup, or go as she was.

Jackson had only checked the clock on the microwave six times as he came and went from the kitchen. He told himself he wasn't nervous and reminded himself people had been late before.

Heck, he was twenty years late for Finley. He figured he could wait an extra twenty minutes for her and their night together. Fair was fair.

And, she was busy, he knew that. He'd experienced the farm and what it was like to get immersed in even the simplest task. So, he'd wait. And he wouldn't check the clock again – after one more time.

Twenty-one minutes.

Finley had changed and put on some riding boots and a lovely cream sweater, then couldn't resist freshening her mascara and blush – she was right there after all – before she ran out the door. It took less than three minutes to run to the cabins and reach number ten, but that didn't stop the slush from splashing up the tall boots or for her to be entirely out of breath by the time she knocked on the door.

"Hi," Finley said, panting and laughing through her ridiculous gasps. "I'm sorry...I'm late. Got. Caught. Up."

The crooked grin Jack offered told her she was forgiven and that the sight alone was worth every tardy minute.

Jack moved aside and covered his laugh with his hand while inviting her in. How could he possibly be anything but happy after it looked like she'd sprinted the entire way there?

"Don't be sorry at all. Where did you come from?" Jackson asked, wondering if she'd run one block or one mile.

The hesitant look she shot him only made his smile grow, and he knew it wasn't as far as she thought it should have been, considering how out of breath she was.

"Well, never mind that. Can I get you a drink? Wine, a winter spritzer, a gallon of water?" He peeked over his shoulder at the last offer and was rewarded with a playful punch on his arm.

"Wine sounds wonderful right now," Finley admitted, to taste and to let her thoughts settle. "And I'd love a glass of water. I came from the farmhouse, judge if you want to."

Jack put up his hands. "I haven't run on purpose in probably a decade. I'm in no place to judge."

When Jack handed Finley a glass of a pretty burgundy red, she inhaled and sipped, and realized she smelled more than the wine. "What is that smell? It smells like savory comfort food."

"Is savory comfort food a good thing?" Jack held the wine bottle frozen over his glass as he waited for her answer.

"It's an extremely good thing. What is it?"

"It's a perfected family recipe, made famous by my grandma. Really fancy." Jack took a sip of his wine. "It's called Chicken Hot Dish."

The way she laughed, freely and lovingly, was enough for him to know he wanted to hear it forever.

"For something so fancy, it's surprisingly secretive in its naming convention. But if it smells this good, I'm not going to turn it away."

"Good, because it's the one thing I know how to make. Oh, and I know how to heat frozen dinner rolls. And what dessert lacks in originality, I feel will be made up for in ambiance – you'll just have to trust me. I should stop talking before you decide to leave."

Finley was more touched by his words and effort than she would have been had he tried to make a six-course meal. She shook her head, grinned, and raised her glass. "To a beautiful winter night, hot dish, and what's already a great night."

"To a great night." Jackson touched his glass to hers and couldn't think of a place he'd rather be more.

However generic it seemed - and how nervous it made him, Chicken Hot Dish was a success. The frozen dinner rolls were warm, fluffy, and topped with butter and honey, and the perfect pairing to the dish. The only thing better was the ease in each other's company and the enjoyment of sharing a winding, entertaining conversation. The flow and drift of it effortlessly moving from one to the other.

Jackson was pleased he let go of the idea of telling her who he was after the first two minutes together. He realized if he would have had that on his mind he'd have missed out on what Finley was actually saying. Her looks were distracting enough. He didn't need twenty-year-old broken promises adding to the distraction. From then on it felt as natural as if they'd had dinner together hundreds of times.

When they finished, they cleared the dishes that came stocked with the cabin and loaded the dishwasher to the sound of Christmas music humming in the background. It was just the break they needed from eating, and with the fire blazing, enough to warm them up for dessert.

Jackson moved to the fridge and pulled out a plate full of white, dark, and milk chocolate bars, marshmallows, and graham crackers.

"Ready for dessert?" he asked, looking at Finley's eyes as they brightened with the sight.

"Absolutely," she said, more excited than she realized she would be for dessert. "What can I help with? And where are we going to roast those?" she asked, eyeing the mallows.

"Let me show you. Let's get you suited up for the outdoors, then you can take this plate. I'll get the rest."

"The rest?" Finley questioned but didn't hesitate to slide on her jacket, hat, and mittens. She tugged on her books as she watched Jack move throughout the room.

First, he gathered two long pokers Finley recognized as belonging to the cabin. Then he pulled two mugs out of the fridge, put them in the microwave, and started it up. Finally, he walked to the fireplace that had been burning since she first walked in and picked up two blankets she hadn't realized had been warming just in front of the hearth.

The idea that he took the time to heat the blankets had her heart soaring. The care he'd taken to prepare for their night added to the warmth spreading throughout her body. Hugging her body to hold the feeling, she wasn't sure she'd even need a blanket where she assumed they were going.

When they stepped outside, Finley cradling the plate full of s'more fixings. She only laughed a little as she watched Jack juggle everything else – including dropping the blankets once along the way.

As they prepared, she imagined there would be a simple fire right outside the backdoor of the cabin. She had been wonderfully wrong.

There was already shoveled path that led to the edge of the pond they had sat at only days earlier watching the sunrise. Where Finley stood now, she could see a fire blazing bright and a single pine tree wrapped in colorful Christmas lights.

Unable to control the gasp of excitement, she asked, "When did you do all of this?"

"For some strange reason Blair only had me scheduled until four today. I had a lot of time on my hands." He nodded to their destination, "This is what happened. Do you like it?"

"Like it? It's – it's like a winter heaven. Let's go. I want to see it!"

Jack could barely keep up with her long, delighted strides.

"This is unbelievable!"

Finley set the plate on the small table she assumed Jack had brought down with the two wooden chairs that sat on either side of it. Both chairs lounged comfortably in the snow, welcoming whoever was to sit there with thick, furry blankets already draped across the seats.

She smoothed her hand over the soft plush material and felt that it, too, had been warmed by the fire. And though it wasn't overdone, she turned to take in the tree Jack had draped in lights, and again to look at the fire. She paused for a moment to hear it crackle and watch the sparks pop and show off their reflection on the ice of the pond. Then she turned to Jack, who was standing, just watching her.

"It's perfect." Finley shrugged out the whisper, not knowing what else to say. No words seemed affectionate enough to describe how endearing and perfectly lovely it was.

Jackson took in her words after noticing every move and every detail of her actions when she reached their destination. Every one of them in childlike awe, every one of them innocently beautiful, and every moment of it was breathtaking. He realized he would be willing to do this for her every night, for the rest of their lives, if it meant she would feel like she did right now. And knowing that she would be his for just as long.

"I'm glad you like it," he finally said, moving first to the table to set down their canisters of hot chocolate and the roasting sticks, then to her to take her hand. He ushered her to her seat and fanned the blanket out, letting it fall around her. He did the same for himself before readying their marshmallows and settling in for another round of conversation.

When she asked more about his job, he openly confided he didn't find the love in it he once had. He shared stories of going on adventures with his brothers as a young boy and dreaming of one day working at their dad's company so they could do it forever.

"I don't know if it was the time with my brothers or the challenge of the great outdoors." Jackson deepened his voice and slowed to flex and joke about how manly they all had been, earning a laugh. But those were some of the best times in my life. I had no idea it would change so much. Though," he said, looking over and catching her eyes, more serious now, "I suppose the youthfulness of it all couldn't last forever. Now I'm stuck in an office having to make decisions that are bigger than myself and it's hard. Really hard. Maybe I just set myself up for failure imagining it would always be like that - when we were bigger decisions, pausing to finish the bite of her white chocolate s'more and wanting to say that as of tonight, she knew exactly what he was talking about. "No, I was like that, too. I understand exactly what you're saying. I used to love every minute of living and working on this farm. One day," Finley's mind drifted to the day of her eleventh Christmas when she realized a promise made a year earlier had been broken. She closed her eyes and decided to keep it to herself – at least for now, "something changed. The magic, the enchantment of it – here – just slowly crept away."

She shrugged at her admittance but realized what she once thought lost entirely, this year, had returned.

"But, this year, something's changed." Finley felt a bashful smile appear at what she was about to say. "When you showed up – you and Nick – things started to shift. What used to be monotonous, what had me questioning the future of the farm, slowly started to vanish. Suddenly I'm noticing winter sunsets, humming to my old favorite holiday albums, and practically skipping through the snow."

Finley stopped only to let her fingers intertwine with his when he offered.

"I'd like to believe it wasn't a coincidence," she admitted.

Jackson gently squeezed her hand, feeling like it wasn't, like Christmas magic had lent a hand in his being there, and said, "It's not."

The feeling of their hands linked had them hoping that the night wouldn't end. But as they both knew, time would move on as the years before had. But it didn't keep them from hoping that their days together would last forever.

CHAPTER 13

Finley finally skipped down the stairs after she saw the lights of cabin ten go dark. Jack was on his way to the bakery, and though they'd just had a date the night before, she couldn't wait to see him that morning. But, she had one stop to make on the way.

Swinging into the kitchen, Finley caught Blair dribbling the last droplets of the gorgeous smelling brew out of the coffee carafe and into her travel mug.

Blair looked up with a guilty smile on her face. "I'll just make another pot." She decided the playful look on her cousin's face didn't call for a serious morning. "But I'm not sharing what's in here, and you already look like you're awake and chipper enough without it. How was your date?" A teasing eyebrow accompanied the question.

"The date was fine," Finley said, as she slowed to a saunter and casually took a seat at the table as Blair cautiously joined her. "I mean, by perfect date standards, it was probably average. You know, like an eleven out of ten." The slow smile crept to her face and Blair slapped a hand on the table then leaned in.

"I knew it! You two are way too perfect for each other. It's like you draw each other in. Understand each other. And look unbelievably beautiful standing next to each other. Oh, the babies you'll have. *So* cute!" Blair swooned.

"Whoa, whoa. Hold on there, lady." Finley reached across and swiped the mug Blair forgot she was hoarding and took a sip. "Let's just start with 'great date' and we'll see how things go from there."

"Fine." Blair stole her mug back. "But just because I'm not saying it doesn't mean I'm not thinking it."

It was too much for Finley to keep her straight face, so she let the happy flutter of laughter escape. *And* because she wanted to share her good mood with Jack, she decided to get down to business.

"The *real* reason I stopped in the kitchen today, after giving up all hope of coffee, is that I saw my agenda."

"Oh, is something wrong? I can move people around, or do you need time off?"

"No, no. I noticed I had two o'clock open. I was wondering what your schedule looked like?"

Blair gave Finley a sideways look and questioned, "Why?" She worried she might be signing herself up for something that wasn't all that great. Blair had the hour open, but wasn't willing to admit it quiet yet.

"Well, are you ready to present your ideas for the farm?"

"What? I mean – I, really?" Blair's excitement was getting the better of her usually confident character. "I mean, yes!"

The animation in her cousin's face was nearly as good as the emotion in her voice. If for no other reason than seeing Blair in an excited frenzy, listening to her pitch her ideas would be worth it.

"Perfect. I'll meet you in the office at two then?"

Blair attempted to compose herself with a cleansing breath, and said, "Yes, two. I'll be there."

As Finley walked out she heard the stifled squeal come from the kitchen and wondered if the day could have started any better.

Then she opened the back door and saw Jack standing outside, his hand raised, ready to knock.

Even through her startle she noticed his grin, his day-old stubble fighting against the boyish dimple that formed, and how his eyes widened at the sight of her. And just like that, the day got even better.

"Jack, hi. I mean, good morning. How are you?" Finley wondered how you greeted a man you had clearly fallen for, whom she just had the most amazing date with, but still had so much to learn about?

"Good morning to you too. You look beautiful."

On his words, unable to help himself, he slowly leaned in and gently pressed his lips to her cheek.

Finley closed her eyes. The snow whirled around her, savoring the moment, as if the years played back as if in an old film reel. In a breath she was ten years old again and a young boy was doing the same. She felt the magic of Christmas consume every inch of her, the joy, the wonder.

Not wanting to open her eyes, wanting to hold the moment forever, she wondered, *could it be?* It was a simple kiss on the cheek, no different than any she'd been given before. But why now, why this one, did it feel so familiar? Why did the past rush through her?

As he pulled back, Jackson read the animated emotions written on her face as if he was reading his favorite book. Did she remember? Would she ask?

"I – thank you," Finley started, searching for an answer in his eyes. Not wanting to say the wrong thing, or be wrong in her feelings. Or, she thought, desperately wanting it to be true, she kept the moment to herself, just for now. "You do, too. Look beautiful, I mean."

It was a lot to take in, he knew. A lot of feelings – old and new. And time; so much time had passed. For now, he'd let it linger with her.

"I thought, if you were headed in my direction, I could walk you to the bakery. What do you say?" he asked, extending an elbow, hopeful she'd join him.

"Well look at the two of you," Maeve quipped as she watched Jackson hold the door open for Finley, then guide her inside. "If the worms weren't frozen, you two early birds would get them. What's the morning order today?"

"Hot–" both Finley and Jack spoke in unison and laughed before Finley took over. "Two hot chocolates, please, and two coffees. I'll have a cinnamon roll. And a bite of whatever this guy's having."

Jackson couldn't deny he liked the way it sounded when she ordered as if they were two, rather than one. He nodded and said, "Gingerbread scone for me. Thanks."

"Anything for you. Be right back."

It didn't take long to shed their winter gear and settle in with the warm drinks Maeve brought out. And when she sat to join them the morning got even better.

"What's on your plate today?" Maeve asked, then added, "Pun absolutely intended."

"I'm going to hang out with Santa Claus." Finley said it as if she'd won the luck of the draw.

"You do know it's field trip day?"

"Field trip day?" Jackson asked.

"Field trip day," Maeve confirmed. "A day when weary teachers, over-sugared children, and brave parent chaperones flock to the farm to sit with Santa, make an ornament, eat lunch, and take a sleigh ride. The only mammal that," Maeve glanced at Finley who was still beaming but went with her thought anyway, "hates this day more than every worker, are the horses."

"Why do they hate it?" he questioned.

"Oh, they don't actually hate it. It's lovely and fun," Finley added cheerfully.

Maeve furrowed her brow, wondering what had gotten into Finley that morning, but went with the feeling of the majority.

"Hate it." Maeve went one. "It's complete chaos from nine in the morning straight through one. Once they leave, you'll need a break to catch your breath, then another break so you realize you're on a break."

"You won't." Finley tried to reassure him. "Where are you stationed today?" she asked Jack.

"I'm on sleigh rides. I figured I was getting a leisure day and would sit and talk to customers while making sure nobody fell off along the way."

"Oh, you'll be making sure nobody falls off, that's for sure. You'll also be counting, wrangling, and making sure nobody takes a detour at the top of the hill and never comes down."

Jackson gulped, wondering if he should really be the one in charge of something like that.

"She's just giving you a hard time. It's going to be fun. The kids love it. And Trish and Carl - they run the rides, remember? They've done this for years. They'll make sure everything goes smoothly. I think Blair is up there with you for a bit, too. Imagine what it would have been like, the excitement you would have had, if you had taken this field trip as a kid?"

The idea held some appeal. He had to admit, he would have loved it – at any age. It would have seemed like they had traveled to the North Pole. "You know, you're right. I think I'm going to love it."

"Another one bites the dust." Maeve got up from the table, clearing their breakfast plates and taking the empty hot chocolate mugs with her. "Well, I'll see you in here for lunch. Then you can tell me if you're singing to a different Christmas tune."

Then she mumbled, mostly to herself, "Crazy love-blinded bluebirds."

"What a day this is going to be!" Nick clapped his hands together and rubbed them in excitement. "All these young and brilliant believers. You know," he said now, looking directly into Finley's amused eyes, "I think that's what makes Christmas so special, why people love it so much. Christmas has a way of bringing us back to a time – maybe even a single moment – that we'll remember forever. It's too precious for us to forget."

Finley saw the twinkle in Nick's eye, then immediately thought of the best day she'd had on the farm. Ten years old, receiving a kiss from a young boy. Then again today, how the memories had rushed back. How wonderfully strange that Nick would have brought something like this up today. But then again, she supposed, not so strange at all considering they were going to be surrounded by children who share that innocent age.

"It is something, isn't it?" Finley asked, but mostly to herself as she placed a hand on her cheek. She looked at Nick, who in that moment seemed more like the real Santa Claus than hired worker, and saw him peacefully smiling in her direction. As if waiting for her to continue.

She wondered, as she felt the warmth from Jack's kiss that morning, if it was possible this was the year she could stop waiting? Was Jack that young boy? What kind of Christmas magic would that be, after all these years?

"Hey Nick," Finley started as she began to hear the excitement and laughter of young children build from behind the shop doors, "I mean, Santa?"

"Yes, dear?"

As the heavy wooden doors pulled open Finley grinned at the sight and decided it could wait. "Never mind, we've got work to do."

On cue, Santa Claus let out a hearty *ho-ho-ho* and what was left of the hoard of children's restraint was lost. Some ran to him to give him a hug, others approached more tentatively, but all captivated by the charm of the old, jolly man.

Finley watched as Santa bent down to rest his hands on his knees as he spoke to each one. She watched him close his eyes as a young girl asked for a hug and he embraced her like a loving grandfather would their granddaughter.

The sight was so touching she nearly teared up, but held back as the teacher and chaperones found her and began asking her for instructions on how she'd like the children to go through the line.

Thoroughly exhausted would be one way to describe how she felt after three hours of wrangling, guiding, coaxing, and persuading what were now starving kids. Luckily, by the time she'd shuffled her last group to the bakery and outdoor seating area, the food was ready and waiting for them. And though she longed for a break, she couldn't deny the rich and fulfilled feeling she had had her walking the grounds.

Initially Finley didn't have a plan, she just wandered away from the crowd for a little quiet, but found herself moving toward the base of the hill where the sleigh rides loaded and unloaded their passengers.

The horses were magnificent as they trotted through the snow to make their last drop off of the morning. It's as if they knew they were every bit as magical as the experience of dashing through the snow for their riders. Their regal black manes waving and their white-socked feet, stepping high even as they made their final clips and came to a stop. From there they'd get fed, pampered, and take a well-deserved rest – but not before being adored, pet, and treated with apples and carrots by the kids brave enough to get close to the elegant, commanding creatures.

Finley walked to the front of the horses and gently stroked the neck of Strudel, her favorite horse.

"You did good today, girl. Almost done. Then Carl and Trish will take you in and spoil you rotten." Finley reached to her right and rubbed the nose of Strudel's companion. "You too, Spritz. You've earned yourself a nice break."

Walking along the side of the sleigh she saw Jack's head poke over the edge and wave to her as if she'd been away for longer than a morning. The gesture caused her heart to swell, then she heard his voice.

"Do they ever talk back?" Jack's eyes gleamed.

Finley lifted her hand to shield her eyes from the sun as she looked up. "Usually, but only when nobody else is looking. How'd it go today?"

"Give me ten minutes and I'll let you know. If we get everybody off without incident, it will have been a success, but I don't want to jinx it. Be right back!"

Without another word, Jack was out of sight. When she moved to the back she watched Jack help the heap of kids to the stairway next to the sleigh so they could safely depart. When he joined in the chant, as they all sang *'Food. Food. Food,"* on repeat, all she could do was shake her head, because she too was feeling famished.

Jackson hopped off the last step as if it was the first time he'd unloaded for the day. But his clothing and boots told a different story.

"You know, I've noticed your clothes aren't quite as new and your boots are a little more ragged. You actually kind of look like a farm-hand."

"Here's to hoping. And if you're tallying, I'm also less sore."

"Ah, so you've passed the final test. Looks like you've earned lunch."

"Do I get to eat with you?"

"I was hoping you might."

Without hesitation, Jack took her gloved hand in his and started to walk with her toward the bakery

"Look at you two, hand-in-hand, smiles on your pretty faces. Still wearing those rose-colored lenses, I see." Maeve winked and threw a hand on her hip. "Now, seeing as I think you've earned it, since all these kids are talking about is Santa Claus and sleigh rides, what can I get you both for lunch?"

"Water. A huge water," Finley started, "and whatever the soup is today with a giant chunk of that good crusty bread you make."

Maeve nodded. "It's a cauliflower cheese chowder today. You could've done worse."

"Mmm, that sounds *so* good," Finley said, her mouth watering at the thought.

"And you?" Maeve looked to Jack.

"The same on the soup. And the biggest whatever kind of sandwich you have."

The smirk that came to Maeve's face showed her approval in Jack's trust in her to pick a great sandwich.

When they were left alone, both let out a sigh, welcoming relaxation. Even the thought of their next task or meetings paled in comparison to the morning. Though neither felt the need to complain.

Finley thought of what Santa had told her about children loving the holiday; about believing. How could she possibly complain at the excitement they held, causing their rambunctious and sometimes crazy behavior. All in all, the kids were perfectly childlike.

Reading her mind, Jack looked over and agreed with the day. It had been great so far – why waste a perfectly good evening to go right along with it?

"Hey, I saw there's a double-feature tonight. *The Santa Clause* and *Elf.* How about date number two?" Jack asked, then worried it may be too much too fast. "If, that's something you'd be interested in. You know, since we, well, just yesterday…"

"I think a movie sounds fun. Pick me up at the farm at five-thirty? Maybe we could grab dinner?"

Jackson couldn't help the ear-to-ear smile plastered on his face. "Dinner and a movie – or two – then."

When two waters were handed to them over the counter, they clinked their glasses and guzzled. Finley hoped her nervous blush wasn't showing – but oh, the feeling Jack gave her. A comfort, a peace, a familiar sense of appreciation. She felt it in his looks, his gestures, and in the way he made an effort to be around her. In the way he took her hand. How could she not get carried away?

The familiar warmth came to her cheek. For the first time she didn't miss the kiss she'd received twenty years earlier, and she didn't wonder if it was him, she was only excited for the opportunity to feel it again.

Christmas carols welcomed Finley into the farmhouse office. Their tunes quietly playing in the background, and a fresh pot of coffee waiting on the table in the center of the room with two of her grandmother's Christmas mugs sitting next to it. The sight was enough to draw a well of water to her eyes but a smile to her face. The gesture was sweet, she thought, just like her cousin.

Two folders lay neatly in front of each chair. One red and one green. Each with bold text on the front that read, *Winter Haven Spread the Joy Project.*

If she wasn't already willing to agree to whatever the girl had to offer, her enthusiasm and love for the farm and the season probably would have been enough. She'd listen intently to what Blair had to offer, but already had an inkling she knew which way she'd fall when it came right down to it.

"Hi! Finley. You're a little early," Blair rushed on, "which is great. Totally okay. I'm ready. Coffee?"

"I'd love some. And grandma's mugs." Finely said, feeling nostalgic as she lifted to inspect the red cardinals resting on flocked pines. "These are still my favorite."

"Mine, too. Whenever I miss her I pull them out. I saw grandpa using one the other day. It was sweet."

"They were sweet."

"Weren't they."

Both of the women sighed then Blair got down to business.

"Ready?"

"As I'll ever be."

Blair took Finley through two options for expansion and covered more detail for each than Finley would have needed to make a final decision that day.

The first was to use their expanded acreage and collaborate with a local company to set up tree sales on site. The second was to take their sales online. Streamline all processes, make all of what they offer available – everything from Christmas trees, to ornaments, to the food they sell in the bakery.

Finley looked at the individual presentations side-by-side, compared the numbers.

"Both of these require additional headcount."

"Yes. All of which are detailed on pages fifteen and sixteen."

"And it looks like we'd need an Operations Manager. Somebody that could maintain the additional business, staff, and logistics."

"All of those decisions, completely up to you. But," Blair wanted to make sure Finley didn't feel the burden of the extra work, "I would do all of the leg work. Find you candidates, vet them, schedule the interviews. Everything."

Finley nodded.

"Has Maeve caught wind of this?" Finley asked, knowing Maeve had a way of wriggling her way into business before it was intended to be shared.

"If she knows, it's because of her voodoo. But I'll do the same for her expansion. She'll obviously need help."

"Yes, she will," Finley confirmed, not wanting to share good news on her friends' behalf.

The coffee was gone, both having had their share of the entire pot. Each tired from the nearly three-hour discussion – though it showed in different ways. Finley stretched and longed for a nap, quickly deciding she deserved one. Blair hopped up and tried to do what she did best – stay busy.

Jack stomped his boots off on the mat outside then let himself in when nobody had answered his knock. He didn't want to be unprepared for the movie, so he also plopped down the bag of blankets he'd packed for the double feature. No snow in the forecast, but that didn't mean they wouldn't be sitting on the frozen ground or leaning against snowy hay bales.

Wandering in, he looked around and called for Finley. Not getting a response, he shrugged and walked around the main level of the farmhouse.

Every inch of it had been decorated for Christmas. There were Christmas trees in the office and the living room, each looking as if they'd been professionally decorated, at least from a distance. But as he closed in on the massive tree tucked between two leather chairs in the main room, he saw nearly all of the ornaments were handmade. Many of them had sloppy names and years written on the bottom and others held grade school pictures of children with missing teeth. It's what the tree at his parents' house had looked like, a tree that belonged in a home.

That's how he felt here – at home.

He moved passed a long dining table, and found the kitchen. It had been updated over the years, but it still felt cozy. All of the dishrags and towels were in creams, reds, and greens, and sitting behind the glass-paneled cabinets were Christmas tumblers, plates, and bowls.

It was as if they transformed the entire house for the season, and, he thought, it matched the spirit of the farm – all happy and full of memories.

Wandering back to the office he decided to wait out his time where he didn't feel like he was intruding. Jack took a seat at the table in the middle of the room and glanced down at the red folder in front of him.

"Winter Haven Spread the Joy Project," Jackson said, smiling at the name while he flipped the cover open, unable to control himself.

With the name assigned to the folder, he figured he was peeking in on something light, something fun. Maybe a charity project or donation. What he found was anything but.

He didn't intend to scan the entire document but after the first page he was pulled to the next, then the next. He wanted to know more. He wanted to see numbers, execution, timelines – and he was given all of it. Jackson's finger flew from line to line as he read.

"This could work," he mumbled to himself, wondering how he hadn't thought of it himself. Though, his presentation wouldn't have been as detailed. "Blair must have put this together."

Taking out his phone he snapped a couple pictures to share with his brothers, then closed the file. If they were on board, it would be the perfect partnership. And something like this might keep him invested, intrigued. He already loved the space, the feel, the work – why not expand on that? And how great would it be to be able to offer Finley and Blair, somebody who was already willing to join them on this project. It practically screamed community, outdoors, wilderness. It was perfect.

Jackson was still riding high when Finley came prancing in. She screamed when she realized she wasn't alone then laughed as she calmed herself, placing a hand over her heart as if to help slow it. Jackson grinned, loving the good nature and carefree in Finley.

"I don't often have that effect on people, it's nice to see I can still stop a heart." He smiled at himself.

"I bet you've stopped a heart or two in your day." Finley sat across from him at the table. "You're far too handsome."

Jackson couldn't help but look into her eyes. "I can only count one time when I think I've truly stopped a heart. And it's a day I've never forgotten."

Finley stared, then gave a slow nod. "I–me too." It was all she could say when words failed her.

"And she reminds me a lot of you. Only I think this time, it's my heart that's stopping." He paused, waited for her to say something – anything. When she didn't, he reached across the table for her hand and said, "I'm ready for heart-stopping."

Not knowing if she had her answer or if she was more confused than ever, Finley simply agreed and placed her hand in his.

"Should we grab dinner?"

He nodded. "Let's do it."

The movie crowd was enough to cover the ground and the hay bales. Finley and Jackson had spread the blankets out, sat close, warming each other. Before the first movie started, both were fast asleep.

CHAPTER 14

They had had an unprecedented almost three full weeks of perfect winter weather. Light dustings of snow here and there to keep the grounds covered, but not too much to keep their customers from enjoying the farm. The wind had been low and the temperature a mild twenty degrees. And though Finley was loving the flurry of people, the joyful interaction, working with her family and friends, and now nightly dates and laughs with Jack, she was ready for the blizzard.

Looking out her bedroom window, Finley could only see the white glow of the ground's lights behind the wall of thick snowflakes. The cabins and the shops were hidden from view and she knew, though they might have a family or two stop by, they would have a day mostly to themselves. The thought almost had her climbing back into bed, but she was up, and as much as sleep sounded wonderful, so did coffee and finding warmth by a fire.

That, *and,* she should probably check on the bakery and make calls to their staff to let them know they didn't have to come in today. What had to be handled could be done by the limited crew onsite. And though Maeve and Miles no longer lived on the grounds, she knew they would have already made the drive in to make sure those one or two customers could fill themselves with the best Christmas eats and treats during their visit.

Leaving her hair long and wavy, knowing there wouldn't be work to be done, she dressed in a comfortable hooded sweatshirt and jeans, then headed down to the kitchen. She heard Blair's voice before she turned the corner and saw the young woman sitting at the kitchen island sipping coffee in her pajamas and robe. Thick, furry slippers hung off her feet, dangling as she swung them back and forth. Finley grinned at the sight and took in the employee checklist and schedule that sat in front of Blair.

The closer she got she saw half of the names and phone numbers were already crossed off the list, and the half pot of coffee sitting in front of her in a large carafe.

When Finley pulled down a mug from the cupboard and slid onto a stool next to Blair, she was greeted with excited eyebrows and a huge smile as she mouthed, "Snow day!" It had Finley chuckling as she filled her own mug. Then Finley picked up her own phone and dialed the next name on the list to tell them to hunker down and enjoy the winter day.

"And, we're done." Blair crossed the last name off the list after she definitively set her phone on the counter. "It's a snow day. I love snow days. But," she looked to Finley, "is there anything you need me to do today?"

"Not a thing. Enjoy a pajama-filled, hot chocolate-drinking, movie-watching, puzzle-making day. Or, I suppose, whatever it is you'd want to do that doesn't involve working. The day is yours."

"It sounds so dreamy. I want to go back to bed just because I can, but then I think, oh my gosh, I have the whole day to myself, I don't want to waste it."

"I understand completely. Don't waste it. Start now, so when you settle in for an afternoon movie you can drift off for a nap without the least bit of guilt."

"No sweeter words have never been spoken. Maybe I can talk gramps into a puzzle. I like that idea." Blair looked at the clock. "It's almost six. He'll be up soon. I'll bribe him with a pancake breakfast, or maybe that blueberry French toast grandma used to make him. He won't not be able to resist."

"Now you're fighting dirty."

"What are you going to do?"

Finley immediately thought of Jack and wanted to spend the day with him, which depended on his schedule, but she could hope. Then she said, "I'm going to head over and hang out with Maeve and Miles for a bit. Schmoose a candied ginger latte out of them, maybe some breakfast, and see where the day takes me. I might be back here showing you and grandpa how to properly put a puzzle together."

"You're on. And just because you stay up until two in the morning to finish puzzles doesn't make you the best – it just makes you crazy."

Finley eyed Blair as her cousin hesitated before going on. Not wanting to press, Finley got up, rinsed the last drop of coffee from her mug, then turned for the door.

"Hey, Lee? Ah," Blair waited for Finley to face her, "I know the decision will take some time, and I know I gave you a lot to consider, but any word on the proposals?"

Finley nodded, smiled. "I gave them a lot of thought. I need a couple more days to run some numbers and look at timing."

Blair tried not to let her shoulders drop at the response but Finley caught the reaction.

"But Blair, I love the ideas. Both of them. *That's* what's taking me so long."

"Really? I mean, okay. Great. Let me know if there's anything else I can do to help."

"I will for sure. Save me a seat at the puzzle table."

"What do we do on a day like this?" Jackson asked Maeve as she brought him a coffee and a scone, then looked outside at the mounting snow.

"Enjoy it," Maeve said, sitting to join Jackson at his table. "We enjoy every single minute of the quiet."

I can do that, Jackson thought, as he took his first scalding sip and wondered if Finley would be willing to enjoy it with him.

"She'll be around," Maeve said, reading his mind as if he'd spoken his thoughts out loud.

"I'm that obvious?"

"Honey, since the minute you laid eyes on her."

"Which time?" Jackson grinned.

"Does it matter?"

"No," he admitted, "I don't suppose it does."

As if on cue, Finley stomped her boots through the door and let a gust of wind and a flurry of snow in with her before she was able to push the door closed behind her.

"Oof – it's a blizzard out there. Literally."

It was the first time Jackson had seen her with her hair down. It was swept over her shoulder to one side, and when she pulled the hood down of her puffy red jacket, it waved loosely around her face. He stood, took her hand, then brushed a strand away from her face.

"Hi," he said, finally.

"Hi, yourself."

There'd been commotion in the back kitchen, but neither Finley or Jack paid any mind to it. They talked and laughed their way through the casual breakfast, loving the simple fact they had no place to be.

When Finley leaned her head back in a genuine belly laugh, her parents who had come in the back entrance of the kitchen, couldn't help but comment. They'd intended to greet Maeve and Miles first thing upon their return after hearing the good news, but didn't expect to find such a jovial crowd.

"My goodness. Have you ever seen her like this with *any* other man?" Fran asked nobody in particular.

All four of them were peeking around the corner to get a good look.

"I don't know if I've seen her like this *ever.*" Maeve added, knowing she'd probably been privy to more of Finley's love life than her parents.

"Hmm," Charlie considered, trying to imagine a time when his daughter had looked at a man the way she was now. A piece of him seeing his little girl, another seeing a beautiful woman, "I don't know, she used to get pretty excited about winter season, and Christmas morning was a close second."

Maeve knew better. This was different. And as she looked at Fran when she started to speak, she saw Fran understood as well.

"This is different. This is love." Fran knew her husband and Finley shared a special bond, but she also knew her daughter, and what she was seeing now was pure happiness. If there was anything better in the world for a mother to see, she didn't know it. And she had to meet the man that was causing it – right now. "I'm going in."

Charlie and Maeve practically tumbled into the open when Fran moved. They straightened and moved in, hoping their commotion wasn't seen.

"It may only have been a couple weeks, but I miss my girl so much when we are gone."

"Mom!" Finley shot out of her chair and tackled her mom in a hug. "When did you get in? There's a blizzard out there." Finley pulled her mom back to look at her at arm's length. "You should be more careful."

"Says the daughter to the mother," Fran said, smiling and talking to Jack who had stood offering his own friendly smile in return.

"We only had to slow down the last two hours of the drive."

"Dad." Finley softened at the sound of her dad's voice and watched him enter the room behind her mom. His hug was next, and though her mom had said it, she too missed them during the weeks they were gone.

"I see how I rate, you coming to see Maeve before me." Finley flung an arm over Maeve's shoulder and accepted the furrowed brow from her mom.

"You know good and well why we had to stop here first."

"I do." Finley squeezed and let go when she saw Jack standing in adoration at the familiarity and love. "Mom, Dad," she said, getting their attention and stepping over to Jack, "This is Jack. He's, well–" how was she supposed to introduce him? Employee? Boyfriend? Handsome man who'd basically swept her off her feet? Her early gift from Santa?

Jack stepped toward Charlie, offering his hand. "I'm new to the winter crew this year. And I've been lucky enough to spend time with your beautiful daughter. I'm really happy to meet you."

Charlie gave Jack's hand a friendly shake. When moved toward Fran, Jack's hand was ignored and he was pulled into a hug one could only describe as a suffocating-mom-hug.

"We are thrilled to meet you, too." Fran moved back and forth in the embrace, holding on just a bit too long as most caring moms did. "I can't wait to hear all about you. What are you two up to today?"

Jack and Finley looked at each other, wondering the same.

Then Finley piped up, "I suppose it depends on how Jack feels about puzzles."

They had all trudged through the snow to the farmhouse and worked their way through a second breakfast of blueberry French toast with Grandpa and Blair, a fresh pot of coffee, dishes, and were well into securing all of the edge pieces to their puzzle.

Fran had caught everybody up on their trip to the Carolinas; the delicious meals they ate, the friends they'd seen, and the weather they loved.

"Though it just isn't winter without snow." Fran ended on the same words that always followed their adventures in retirement.

When Jack's phone rang and he stepped away, nobody commented on his departure, they simply continued working on the puzzle in silence – shifting their eyes back and forth to everybody but Finley – until she noticed.

"What?"

Fran shrugged defensively. "What do you mean, what?"

"I see all of you sending your telepathic signals. Spit it out." Finley pointed a puzzle piece to everybody at the table.

"It's just, Jack?"

Finley tried to hide her sheepish grin. "What about him?"

Blair leaned back. "You might as well talk; your face is giving you away and your cheeks match the cranberry in the garland."

Leaning over to glance down the hall where Jack had moved to take his call, Finley whispered, "I don't know what you want me to tell you. I like him, probably very much. But he's a seasonal farm-hand. I don't know what his intentions are beyond his temporary employment."

"Really." Blair wasn't satisfied. *"That's* what you have to say for yourself?*"

"Really, and shh."

Charlie shifted in his chair to ease his stiffening muscles from holding his position over the puzzle and, he supposed, hours of riding in a car. Then he commented, "I think something could be arranged where his employment wouldn't have to be temporary. You know as well as anybody another full-time employee wouldn't be a bad thing."

The thought had crossed her mind, but hearing her dad say it out loud only solidified why she hadn't broached the subject with Jack. "I know. But he already has a job. He works for his own family's company. He's only here to help out. Then he has to go back."

Fran had watched Jack closely throughout the morning. From what she had seen, he didn't look like a man who wanted to walk away from the farm – or Finley. "Well, it's something to keep in mind. You never know where people's hearts truly lie."

"Yeah," Finley murmured, considering her mom's words, "you never know."

Jack moved down the hall to the back of the house to use the office. When he saw Jake's name scrolling across his phone he knew he had to answer, and for the first time in a long time, he wanted to.

"Did you get my email?" Jackson asked, trying to sound more professional than eager.

"I did, that's why I called."

There was a pause on the line, neither brother spoke.

"I think you're onto something." Jake said, finally. "I, well, I like it. So does James. Dad wants us three to figure it out. He's – starting to step back."

"I figured."

"Okay, when can you come into the office to go through this in detail?"

"Let me get back to you. I have some details to sort out here." Jackson closed his eyes and thought, more like he needed to explain why he knew their plans, then beg Finley to let their company be a part of their new project.

"We need something before Christmas. That gives you seven days."

Jackson rubbed his hand over his face. "Yeah, got it."

"Hey, Jackson," Jake said, sounding less like a business partner and more like his brother, "I know it's been a rough go of it, but this is good. I'm proud of you."

"Thanks, I'll get back to you."

Jackson put the phone down in the middle of the office table and closed his eyes. His weary sigh was audible, and he realized as he let it out that he wasn't the only one feeling fatigue. Jake had sounded just as tired; the year had been hard on all of them.

"Hey you, everything okay?" Finley asked as she stepped into the doorway, leaning her body onto it.

Unable to keep from smiling at the sight of her, he grinned and gave what passed as an extremely passive nod. He knew he no longer loved the job he was doing with his family, but he didn't realize just how much it taxed him until he'd found something he did love. Even the brief call with his brother about this small project was enough to tire him.

"Everything is good – or will be. That was Jake, my brother. Business never stops, even when you're on a temporary hiatus. And at that, do you have a minute to talk business?"

"I do…tomorrow." Finley moved into the room and sat with Jack at the table. "But today, let's enjoy not having to worry about any job or any business dealings. Talk tomorrow?"

What's another day? he thought.

"Deal. What's next on the agenda?"

"The day is yours for the making." Finley brightened. "Though, there's a strong push for Italian almond cookies and a movie."

"Bring it on. But," he added, "I'll not be out-puzzled by your family."

Finley placed her hand over her chest, swooning. "A man after my own heart."

CHAPTER 15

When Finley came down the stairs the next morning she heard the familiar hum of her dad's voice, quietly following the chipper tune of *Santa Claus is Coming to Town.*

Some things never change, Finley thought as she could already picture her dad in work clothes, preparing for a day on the farm.

"I thought there was a rumor going around that you retired a couple years back?" Finley teased as she moved past her dad, who had already brewed a second pot of coffee.

"Is that why I haven't been getting paid? I'm going to have to talk to the boss about that." Charlie grinned and gave his daughter a nudge with his elbow as she joined him at the counter. "Who guzzles all the coffee in the morning?" Charlie motioned to the pot.

Finley followed his gesture and raised an eyebrow. "Blair seems to have gotten the early morning gene that runs in the family. Though her clock is set about an hour ahead of the rest of us. And I thought *we* were the obnoxious early risers."

"I heard that!"

Charlie and Finley swung their heads toward the door in time to see a figure fly by and head toward the office, in enough of a flurry to get laughter out of the both of them.

"Well, if she's hard at work I suppose I can kick up my feet for another ten minutes or so until I head up."

"Head up?"

"Yup," Charlie began, trying his best for casual, "Blair scheduled me on the hill today with Jack. We're on tree duty."

"Oh, she did, did she?" Setting her cup down, Finley leaned forward to give her dad a speculative stare. "That seems pretty convenient."

"It's only convenient if my daughter has romantic feelings for the seemingly good guy. But," Charlie didn't let Finley cut in, "seeing as you're unsure of his future on the farm, or in your life, I like to think of it as just another day on the farm. Two men, doing manly things with chainsaws, axes, and big trucks."

"Think you're so clever." Finley picked up her mug to sip the hot liquid and eyed her dad.

"Lee, there was a time your mother might have said exactly the same thing about me. Thing is, when it's love, it's love. Everybody seems to see it before you do. And, I hate to say this, sometimes it takes realizing they aren't there to know you want them to be."

Saying nothing, Finley continued to listen.

"I did that with your mother, you know. I left for a day. Just a single day. Woke up the next morning and decided I'd never go another day unsure if she were mine or not."

"I didn't know that. What did she do?"

Charlie gave a hearty laugh. "She stood on the steps right outside, watched me pull up in my rusty truck, and asked what took me so long."

"Of course she did." Finley shook her head and grinned at her mom, able to picture the entire scene. "Why tell me that now?"

"Just in case you didn't want to get to the point of wondering if he'd come back if he left. You know, you could tell him how you feel."

"Maybe you are a little cleverer than I give you credit for," Finley said, pushing away from the table.

"Where are you headed?"

"To talk to a guy about some breakfast."

"That's my girl."

There was something about the farm after a heavy snowfall that looked magical. The sun caused the ground to sparkle as if somebody had thrown glitter in the air and let it flutter and fall to rest on the snow. Every once in a while, a small gust of wind would pick up the glittery dust and swirl it in the air; and if you happened to be passing by you could feel the cool speckles sprinkle upon your face.

As Finley walked she took the time to notice the flocks of snow mounded on the wooden fence and lamp posts, how it piled high on the side of the walkway, and how it hung from the top of the shop roofs. As she moved, she stretched her eyes up to the miles of trees on the hill. The view was no longer a deep, forest green, but a glistening white. Pausing at the entrance of the Christmas tree lot, she grinned at the view. It looked especially enchanting with lights strung around the border and all of the trees standing inside, like a charming winter maze.

Even now, after the plows had cleared the roads and the paths for the horses, sleighs, and trucks that would climb the hill, it still looked untouched.

Finley stood at the base of the hill and watched as her dad and Jack made their way up. It must be the first trip of the day. The truck was bright red, not a speck of dirt on it, but that would change come noon – or come the next half hour or so.

Thinking about noon, Finley wondered if she should grab her parents and Blair and talk about business. Get everybody's input on Blair's projects, and so she could tell them about Mr. Jorgenson's offer. She was curious about what they would think and say – though she had an idea of where their hearts would fall when it came to the farm. She was finding her heart landing in quite the same place as of recently.

Wandering a bit more, Finley finally found the old hay bale outside of Santa's workshop and brushed the heap snow off the top with her glove before sitting. It had been weeks since she sat there to think. The last time, her thoughts and her heart had felt so differently. But now, as she looked around, everything looked…happier.

Was it the snow? Had the season finally taken hold and as it did every year? Had it melted her heart and had she found satisfaction in the work once more? Or, Finley looked to the hill, did it have to do with filling a piece of her heart that had been missing?

She'd always been so content, so strong, so determined. She would have done the job and done it well had Jack not shown up with Santa.

Finley couldn't help the small upward twist of her lip now that she'd finally decided Nick was the real Santa Claus; besides, it was so much more fun to believe.

But – she thought as she leaned back, resting her head as she looked out – would she have appreciated it, looked at it through Jack's eyes, saw the beauty and wonder that was the farm, had he not reminded her? And, had it been anybody else, would she have listened?

Jack was man enough to admit coming out to cut trees down after a blizzard was a little bit like playing in the snow – and that he enjoyed it. He trudged through, creating his own paths, dug around the bases with his hands, and got to operate hand tools – is that not every boy, or man's, dream?

After finishing a line of trees, he picked up the bottle of water he had plopped in the snow, and guzzled while he looked at the scene below. He scanned, saw the first signs of life funneling out of cars and making their way down the plowed paths. Kids skipping and parents walking in behind them. As he panned, he paused on a small figure sitting on a hay bale.

He sipped and stared. Jack could watch her all day just like this, wondering what she was thinking, wishing he could be next to her to ask. Wanting to tell her the best day of his life started at that very spot.

Charlie watched Jack for a bit, took note as his eyebrows lifted, and watched the grin form while he took in the farm. He also watched as his eyes settled peacefully on his daughter, and as everything in Jack's body relaxed.

"Not a bad view, is it?"

Jackson knew then he'd been caught, but why do anything other than admit the truth? "It's one I've been looking for for a long time."

"And now that you have it?" Charlie crunched through the top snow and flung the underlying powder with every step as he moved toward Jack.

Jackson grinned and stole a quick look over to Charlie, who had a look on his face that told him he understood. "I'm not sure I'll ever be the same."

"Look at this," Fran said, beaming as she walked a tray full of grilled cheese sandwiches to their dining room table, "all of my favorite people around the table. And in the middle of a work day no less."

Finley and Blair rolled their eyes, knowing they would have made time for the gathering like they had many times before – even on workdays. But then again, nobody could really resist Fran's homemade grilled cheese and tomato soup.

They all inhaled as Fran made her second trip in with a Dutch oven full of the homemade soup.

"Mmm, Mom, that smells so good."

"Then you can have seconds."

Fran had made a point to set out Christmas bowls and serving plates. They were getting too close to the holiday not to be able to celebrate the feeling of it every minute.

She'd lit the forest green pillar candles that sat in the antlers of two bronze reindeer figurines, and lit the fire at the end of the room. Everything about it was cozy, with just the right amount of pretty.

"Since I have you all here," Finley started as everybody took a buttery grilled sandwich before passing the plate to the next person, "I want to let you all know we've had a couple of developments since mom and dad have been away."

Nodding to her dad who offered a ladle full of the fragrant tomato soup, she held up her bowl so he could serve her before setting it down. Finley saw she had her family's attention, though they had all started enjoying their first bites, so she joined them.

Through her first chew, she continued, "I was approached a couple weeks ago by a man, Connor Jorgenson, who was interested in buying the farm."

That got everybody to stop mid-bite and look up with intrigue and surprise.

"And?" Blair, who couldn't – or wouldn't – wait for Finley to finish her bite, urged her on.

"Well," she swallowed, "he offered me – us – seven million dollars."

"He *what?*" Grandpa Chuck said through a gargle, struggling to keep his tomato soup in his mouth.

Blair was curious, "Grandpa, how much did you buy the initial land for when you started it up?"

"I don't know if we have the old registers or not – would be something if we did somewhere – because, I don't remember. But," he said, before everybody could be let down, "I do remember thinking I was being robbed paying eighty bucks an acre."

"Eighty dollars? As in eight-zero?" Blair couldn't believe what she heard.

"Eighty. Boy I wish your grandma could have heard this. She thought I was outside of my mind spending money on an ugly hunk of land. Of course, at the time," Grandpa Chuck laughed, "I had no idea what we were going to do with it. Come to think of it, I can't believe she gave in."

"What would have she done?" Finley couldn't help herself. She wanted to know what her grandmother would have said if she were offered that type of money for their farm.

"Oh, well, she was a savvy business woman and spoke her mind about it. Probably why I loved her so much. That wasn't too common back then – times were a little different."

"Grandma was awesome." Blair nodded with her statement.

"That she was," Grandpa Chuck agreed. "And even in knowing – though I'm making a bit of an assumption here – it's not worth seven million today and that's an extremely generous offer, she still would have turned it down."

Finley watched her parents eye each other and squeeze one another's hand at the words, then looked back to her grandpa. "Why?"

A sentimental look passed over his face. "I think for two reasons. She would have said the farm's time isn't yet over. She'd see the movement, the people, our family of workers, and feel it wasn't time. But mostly, she would have said because this is home. And that, to her, would have made it priceless."

Grandpa Chuck saw the turmoil on Finley's face as he relayed what he thought his late wife's opinion on the matter might have been. He didn't think Finley would agree, but he wanted – for her – to say it out loud.

"What did you tell our friend, Mr. Jorgenson?"

"Ah." Finley flattened her hand through the air and shook her head to indicate her thoughts. "Nothing. I, ah, I told him nothing." She shrugged. "He gave me a business card and after that day I hadn't really thought about it."

But, she thought, hadn't she thought, at the beginning of the season, about a life outside of the farm? A rush of guilt passed through her for having imagined it.

Wanting to leave the subject and her feeling of shame behind, Finley quickly shifted gears. "And, since we are *not* selling the farm, and Blair was blessed with Grandma's good business sense, we have a couple of new ideas to run by you."

Not feeling the burden of anything, only excitement for getting to share her thoughts with her family, Blair was nearly bounding out of her seat as she shared her ideas. Her hands perfectly punctuated every word, as if playing a game of charades as she spoke.

Finley finished her lunch, mostly in silence except when Blair looked to her for approval or comment. Then she moved to the kitchen to help her mom with dishes before heading out again.

When her mom kept stealing glances at her as she dried, Finley decided she couldn't take it anymore.

"What?" Finley said with a huff of laughter.

"Nothing, nothing at all." Fran snapped her attention back to the bowl she was wiping down.

Finley set down the dishrag and turned, showing she'd not do another dish until her mom told her what was on her mind.

"You have to stop."

"Stop what?" Finley expected most anything but a feeling of confusion.

"Stop feeling guilty for considering the offer."

"I didn't consider it."

"Then why the sudden silence and mind-racing at lunch?"

Finley stuck out her lower lip and blew a long breath out. Was she really *that* obvious?

"I was – there was – no." Finley paused to gather her thoughts. "At the beginning of the season I felt tired," she explained. "I didn't know if I wanted to do all of the work; put in the early mornings and late nights. I questioned if *this,"* her arms went wide, "here, was really what I wanted to do for the rest of my life."

Finley waited a beat, then dropped her head before continuing. "Maeve – *God love Maeve* – talked to me and told me to *enjoy* the work. Just go one more season and really appreciate it. Then, if at the end of the year I still felt like I didn't like it, then I could make a decision."

"She has always been a good ear for you. And sometimes an even better voice. You get lost in there sometimes." Fran grinned and swirled her finger around her daughter's forehead. "But, you know," now she took Finley's chin gently between her index finger and thumb, "you are free to make whatever decision you like. Yes, I think talking about it with the family is good and right, but you – and Blair – you girls are not tied to this place. You owe it, and you owe your father and I, and your grandpa, nothing. If selling was what everybody really wanted in the end, you could have done that. And," Fran smiled, "we all would have been just fine."

Fran gave a final squeeze of her hand then returned to drying, so Finley did the same and picked up a new dish to wash. After a moment she said, "Thanks, Mom."

"You, my precious girl, are so welcome."

Late into the night, after all had dozed during a fireside movie night and finally made their way up to their rooms, Finley picked up empty or half-eaten popcorn bowls and strewn mugs of hot chocolate or glasses of egg nog, and walked them to the kitchen. As she moved in the comfort of her flannel pajamas and thick furry slippers, she didn't realize how much she – and it seemed everybody else – needed a quiet night.

First a snow day, then a silent night. Maybe that's something they'd have to work into the schedule the following year. Mandatory no-work days, where they'd close the farm. It didn't even have to be a full day, but just enough for people to enjoy some family time, or time to themselves during the season.

For now, though, she had more important things to do. She might as well end the great day by making somebody else's.

Finley found Blair prepping the coffee pot for tomorrow morning's brew. She efficiently piled the grounds, set the timer, and nodded to herself when she was done. Without disturbing the process, Finley walked to the sink and placed the dishes in it.

"Okay," Blair said, without looking over, "though I'll deny I ever said this if you speak it to another human, I admit, you are the puzzle master. It took you a day longer than I expected, but your skills are still impressive."

Smiling before she turned to debut her playful but pompous grin, Finley said, "I'll take the compliment to the grave. But, for your admittance, I have something for you."

Intrigued, Blair slid closer to listen.

"Let's go for it."

"Go for it?" Blair questioned, repeating the words almost to herself to try and place them. Then it registered. "Oh my gosh. Oh my gosh! You mean – like – *let's go for it!*"

Yes, Finley thought, perfect ending to the day. Then she confirmed, "Yes, let's do it. *But,*"

"But? But what? Why a 'but?'"

Laughing, Finley accentuated the word, trying to get Blair to listen through her excitement, *"But,* we are going to need somebody to manage the project, and take over that division of the farm."

"Yes, absolutely. I'll start looking right away."

"I already had a candidate in mind."

"Oh? Well, that's even better."

"You."

Blair's eyes shot up. "Wait, you, you mean me?"

"I mean you. If you want it, of course."

"If I want it? If I want it!" Blair jumped into Finley's arms and gave her the biggest hug she could and squeezed until she felt Finley gasp for air.

"Now, if you're up for it, you can run the show. Find the companies, vet them, and narrow them down. I obviously want to be in on the decision – and need to be – but it's your baby, you run with it."

"This is just too much. My head's already spinning – in a good way! I have so many ideas."

Finley watched Blair pace the kitchen in front of her and wondered if her cousin would sleep a wink.

Blair stopped and looked Finley dead in the eye, "I won't let you down."

"I know you won't. You're perfect for this in every way. For the business, and the family."

"Oh! One more thing, ah– which option are we doing?"

"I figured that's up to you. Though I thought a combination of both would be nice."

"All my dreams come true." Practicing a faint with the back of her hand to her forehead, Blair spun into a chair. "I'm going to need a minute."

"If you need more than another minute with me, let me know, otherwise I'm heading to bed."

"No, you're free to go. You've sufficiently made my dreams come true. Love you, Lee."

"Love you, too. Night."

CHAPTER 16

Jake Bloom was a well-built, sharp-dressed man. He, unlike his brother, liked the corporate side of business. Sure, he appreciated the outdoors, the sights, the smells, the struggle that sometimes came along with it. He also was fond of the gear it took to properly enjoy nature, and he definitely liked the profits. He just happened to like walking into his nice office every day and figuring out what it took to make – and keep – a company successful more.

That's probably why he and his brothers usually worked so well together. He was all business, Jackson brought the reality, necessity, and customers' needs to the forefront in their discussions, and James liked the numbers.

A triple threat. Jake thought of the words his dad had said many times before.

Jake grinned at the thought, then at the sight as he walked up to the large iron sign that boasted *Winter Haven.* He couldn't believe it had been so long since he'd been back. What had it been? Nearly twenty years, he would have guessed.

Laughing to himself as he walked under the arched sign, he thought about the grief he'd given his brothers about believing in Santa Claus back then. But, he had to admit, it was a heck of a day.

And, if what Jackson had sent over was a legitimate business opportunity, today was going to be a heck of a day, too.

Blair stood watch in the farmhouse, spotting the slick-looking man who'd gotten out of his car and strolled onto the grounds with casual confidence that wreaked money. *Seven million,* she thought.

He'd caught her eye, as he was unashamedly handsome, but as soon as his distant charm struck her, she knew who he was. Her mood and stature immediately shifted.

With every step he took, eying the shops, judging the cabins, evaluating the acreage, his smug – but admittedly cute – smile grew. And as it grew, her defense of the farm – her family's farm – amplified.

Who was *he* to come here, where they had put their sweat and tears, heart and soul, into this land? Into this beautiful wonderland?

"This winter wonderland that I'm going to help expand so we can share it with even more people, you selfish jerk." Blair muttered to herself, letting her irritation grow.

Sufficiently stirred-up, she marched to the back door, shoved on her boots, jacket and hat, and stalked straight toward him.

As the young woman approached, Jake smiled and held out a hand. It had to be Finley given his brothers' description of her, though he thought she'd be older.

"Hi there," Jake held out his hand, "I'm–"

"I know who you are." Blair's words were clipped as she stopped and gave his hand one hard shake before dropping it.

"Ah, okay. Well, great. You must be–"

"I'm Blair Whittaker, I'm the farm's assistant manager."

"Oh, sure. Sorry about that, I mistook you for somebody else." *A less feisty somebody else,* he thought. Though, he supposed he could see the appeal, for the right person. The way his brother had been talking about this Finley, he half assumed he was in love with her. Well, Blair should at least be able to help him or point him in the right direction. "I'm hoping to talk to Finley Whittaker, is she around?"

Jake pocketed his hands and thought aloud, "And actually, if Jackson Bloom is here, it would be great if he could join us as well."

"She's – wait, Jack? How do you know Jack?"

Even though he found it interesting that Miss Assistant Manager didn't understand why he was here to talk to Finley and Jackson, he obliged. "He works with me. We'd like to discuss a business opportunity."

Blair couldn't believe what she was hearing. *Jack* was in on it? It couldn't be. He couldn't be here just for the sole reason of research. He loved it here.

Blair's eyes grew wide at the thought, *he loved it here.* It was a part of his plan all along. Here she thought he'd shown up in the nick of time, truly fallen for Finley, had basically become a part of their work family – or more. But it was all, for what? *Business?*

No, she wouldn't have it, and she wouldn't put Finley through the same realization – at least not publicly.

"No." Blair said, firmly as she regained eye contact. "Finley is not available, and she's not interested in your offer. This is a family farm, and it will *stay* a family farm for the indefinite, foreseeable future."

Jake blinked at the young woman who'd rightly put him in his place, but stewed on her words. The longer he stood in silence, the more irritated he became with Jackson. Unfortunately, his irritation was going to be directed at Blair.

"I see." He nodded curtly. "Then consider us officially uninterested in your partnership."

Jake started to turn to walk away, then paused and looked over his shoulder. "And tell *Jack* his playtime is over. He needs to get back to work. *Real* work."

Blair let her mouth hang open. *The nerve of that man.* But there was one thing that was worse than being told off by an arrogant jerk; having to tell Finley the man she's fallen for was here under false pretenses.

Jackson looked down at his buzzing phone and rolled his eyes.

"You give the guy one little good idea and he's obsessed with it," Jackson said as he declined Jake's call for the second time. He'd call him back in due time, but right now he was watching Finley slowly high-step through the snow toward the frozen pond from across the farm. Her movements looked practiced, perfected. As if she'd walked the same path a thousand times.

Unable to resist, Jackson dropped his empty paper cup into the trash and followed her.

The sun was dipping down in the early evening of winter, letting a nice sunset reflect off the frozen water. When he saw her, she was sitting in one of the chairs he'd placed at the edge of the pond.

She looked peaceful, content. But mostly, he thought, she looked like she beautifully belonged. And, if he wasn't getting too ahead of himself, he felt he belonged there with her.

"Mind if I join you?" Jackson asked as he approached.

Her smile was casual as she turned toward his voice, her eyes following his movements as he closed the gap between them.

"I'd love for you to join me. I'm afraid I stole your spot, but when I thought of it today during a quick break I couldn't resist walking over."

"It suits you," he admitted. "And I like to think of it as *our* spot. It wouldn't be the same if it wasn't shared."

Finley nodded and turned, expecting him to sit with her. When he didn't she looked up and saw his hand extended in her direction. Upon her questioning look, Jack offered, "Join me for a spin in the snow?"

Leaning her head to the right, Finley grinned and faintly noticed *White Christmas* crooning over the farm speakers. She nodded.

Her hand in his, he pulled her to her feet and held her close. The snow surrounded their feet, shifting and moving, sparkling flakes dusting into the air, as their dance carried them in small circles.

At first Finley searched for words to say, wanting to tell Jack how he was filling her heart, and how she didn't want it to end. But the quiet moment was too special for words. Instead she leaned her head on his shoulder and let him sway her to the music.

When the tune changed and picked up the pace, Jackson couldn't help but pull her with him as he spun, swinging her out and back to him. When her head fell back on a laugh the dizzying spin caught their feet and they both started a tumble to the ground. Finley let a playful screech out as she reached for Jack, a final attempt to catch herself, but all he did was cradle her in and fall on the fluffy powder with her.

Their gasps came from a mixture of cool snow finding its way beneath their warm jackets and the uncontrollable breathless laughter.

After trudging all over the grounds, stalking every building, the tree lot, the movie grounds, and up the hill, Blair finally found what she was looking for.

She stood watching the heart-wrenching scene of Finley and Jack sharing a dance and near film-worthy laughter as they fell to the snow together. Both seemingly having the time of their lives.

Covering her face with her hands she groaned. Then she turned to walk away, only to turn around again – three times. If it was her, if she was in Finley's position, she'd want to know the truth. No matter how hard it would be to hear.

Blair held her arms at her sides, hands in fists, then took a deep breath. On her exhale she studied Jack, the way he looked at Finley, how he took care to brush the snow off of her face, stand and help her to her feet, then bring her in so he could wrap his arms around her.

He probably did have feelings for Finley. Who wouldn't? She was stunning, hard-working, successful, dedicated. Caring to a fault if somebody took the time to get to know her. That's probably why Lee quickly became her role model. Every minute of her childhood consumed with wanting to be so much like Finley.

But facts were facts. She'd lay them out for Finley, and let her decide how she wanted to move forward with her own feelings, because they were quickly moving in the direction of love.

Blair moved through the snow, not bothering to high-step, just plowed each booted foot through the feet of snow in front of her. She didn't look up. She didn't want to see their faces until she was close, though she knew they heard her coming.

"Hey, Blair." Jack waved amiably and Finley radiated happiness through her smile and slight embarrassment of being caught embracing Jack.

"Hi," Blair said, sounding shorter than she intended, but wanting them to know her visit wasn't a pleasant one.

Concern replaced the happiness on Finley's face. She asked, "Blair, what's wrong? Is everything okay?"

Only shaking her head at first, not knowing how to begin, she finally decided she'd just have to say it all. "I learned something today that I have to share with you. What you do with the information is up to you."

"Sure, whatever it is, please say it." Finley dropped her arms from their perch on Jack's shoulders.

"Jack isn't who you think he is."

Finley looked from Blair to Jack, confused at what she was saying.

Jack couldn't stop the instant look of fear that paled his face. *She must know who I am,* he thought. *Twenty years was a long time ago, but that couldn't possibly change their feelings for each other now. It took him too long to get there, sure, but he was here now – that's what mattered.*

"He's the one trying to steal our business." There, she said it.

"I–" Jackson was ready to defend himself but tripped over his words. "What?"

He looked from woman to woman. How could Blair possibly know he wanted to be a candidate for their new partnership? "No," he stuttered, "no, I mean, not steal."

On hearing his stumbling words Finley looked over. "Excuse me? Is what Blair is saying true?"

"No – yes," he corrected himself when Blair's steely eyes bore into him, "not exactly. It's not stealing."

Finley looked to Blair for more.

"Your slick businessman came today, looking at the grounds, nearly salivating. I confronted him, told him we weren't interested in his offer. Then he told me that Jackson could pack up and come back to work. That his play time was over."

Now, having no idea what Blair was talking about, Jackson was completely at a loss for words. He no longer knew how to explain, because he didn't know what he was explaining. *Steal the company?* He racked his brain trying to piece everything together, but they were moving too fast for him.

Finley was already stepping away from him, in obvious disgust. A look of hurt and betrayal on her face, tears threatening to fill her eyes.

"I think you should leave," Finley said at last. Not wanting to hear excuses, and not wanting her feelings to cloud her better judgement.

"I think we need to talk about this, I thought it's what you–"

"Just go." Finley looked away.

Wanted. I thought it's what you wanted, Jackson thought to himself, but didn't say it realizing nothing would help. Apparently, he'd read everything wrong: the project, the opportunity, and to his already noticeable anguish, Finley.

Katie Bachand

CHAPTER 17

"Hey," Maeve said softly, as she moved around the bakery counter. Her eyes fixed on Finley, who sat staring at her untouched cup of coffee in front of her. "You going to be okay?"

Finley said nothing for a moment. She tried to think about how she felt right that moment. Three nights and two full days had gone by since she asked Jack to leave, and in that time, she felt like she experienced more *feelings* than her entire life combined.

She felt betrayal, bitterness, bitter sadness, a sense of loss, felt lost during moments knowing Jack was gone, she felt anger, and now? Now what did she feel? Empty. But, that wasn't the question. The question was, would she be okay?

"Yeah," Finley said, finally. She hated how small her voice sounded.

Knowing Finley wouldn't like being questioned, Maeve tried another avenue. "You know, it's really early, even for you."

"Can't sleep." Finley didn't have the energy to tell Maeve quarter to five wasn't early, if you considered she'd been lying awake in bed since three. But her mind wouldn't shut off. She replayed every moment she and Jack had together and tried to find a single time when she thought he might be deceiving her, but she found nothing. It would have been easier if she could find a crack in his façade. Something that would make him seem unworthy of her love, of her trust.

Then there were all the calls. Finley looked at her phone that sat on the table next to her cup. It seemed every time she thought of him he tried calling her. His messages always saying the same thing, all sounding the same. A pain-filled voice asking for her to answer, to talk to him.

There was nothing to say.

Finley's phone lit up, getting the attention of both women. Maeve looked on hopefully; Finley tentatively looked over as if she was afraid. An audible sigh of relief came from Finley when she saw it was her agenda for the day.

"Where are you headed for the day?" Maeve asked.

Sliding her finger across the screen, Finley studied her day, and decided it was as good a schedule as any. She could avoid most people she knew and the kids would keep her busy.

"Looks like a day with Santa Claus."

Maeve liked the idea of Finley spending the day with Nick. He was sensible, cheerful, and if anybody could work a little Christmas magic on Finley, it was him.

Reaching across the table, Maeve rested her hand on Finley's.

"Try to enjoy it, even though it's hard. And I know it's so hard. It's still a beautiful, happy place."

Finley tried not to get emotional but the tears welled in her eyes. Partly from sadness, but also from knowing what her friend said was true.

But why, then, did she feel like such a big part of the farm was missing? *Why* did she feel like she was eleven years old realizing that her heart was learning what it was like to be broken for the first time, all over again?

Blair sat in the farmhouse office, throwing herself into work – more than she usually did. Something about everything that happened with Jack wasn't sitting well with her. She knew she did the right thing in telling Finley the truth, but there was this little nagging ache that alternated between her stomach and her head. Currently, it sat in the latter.

Rubbing the spot between her eyes she forced herself to focus on the task at hand. If Finley gave her the responsibility to find a good – knowing she'd only settle for great – company to work with, then that's exactly what she'd do.

She researched and vetted what seemed like hundreds of local and multi-state companies. Grocery stores, clothing stores, home décor companies, and sporting goods stores. Nothing seemed right. And if they were going to do this, it had to make sense.

Sitting back in her chair Blair tried to think about the farm, about everything her family – mostly Finley – had turned it into. It was rustic wilderness. It was natural beauty. It was old-world charm and comfort. It was also hard work, and it was real. People didn't come just to pick out a tree, a wreath, or an ornament. They came to cut down a big pine of their own. To make a wreath of evergreen, berries, and pinecones. To find or create an ornament that reminded them of something that wasn't flashy, but about the experience.

Blair clicked her pointer finger on the delete button until her original list of companies was gone. They weren't *it*.

"You look like you're having yourself a day." Fran walked into the office and set a tray on the table.

Blair looked up and saw it held a steaming pot of something that smelled like cinnamon spices and sweet milk.

"Mmm, is that homemade chai?"

"It might be."

"If having a day earned me that, I welcome it. Share it with me?"

"Exactly what I was hoping to do." Fran poured two cups while Blair moved around the desk and joined her at the table. "How are you, honey?"

Falling into the chair, Blair slouched and shook her head, then looked at her aunt. "Honestly?" She wrapped her hands around the mug and stared. "I'm a little deflated. Have you ever done something that felt right and completely wrong at the same time?"

Fran nodded, knowingly. "Usually when it had to do with a hard truth. There were times when I was right, and didn't want to be. And times when I was wrong, and thankful for it. But," Fran continued, as she watched Blair's struggle, "I don't regret any one of them because at the time I did what I thought was right."

"I assume you know by now I'm the one who told Finley about Jack?"

"I do." Fran's words were calm and free of blame.

Blair nodded. "If you were me, or in my shoes, what would you have done?"

"Hmm, well," Fran thought for a moment. "I think if it meant protecting somebody in my family I would have done close to the same thing."

"Close?"

"Oh sure. I would have told Finley, but I do think I would have dug into the details a little more. I'm surprised with your zealous nature – in an admirable way," Fran grinned, "– you didn't. Or perhaps you did and found the hard truth I mentioned earlier?"

Blair felt the blush rise in her cheeks. She didn't look into it. And her aunt was right, normally she would have dug, scraped, and clawed every detail she could have out of Jorgensen and Jack Bloom. Then why didn't she this time? Was she afraid she'd find perhaps she was wrong? Or, worse. Find she was right? Either way, she dropped her head, she knew in the moment she had let her emotions get the best of her.

"I haven't – or, not yet." She decided right then she'd work time into the next couple days to look into it. Christmas was nearly upon them and the customer rush would slow, freeing up her time. She owed that to Finley, and to herself. "I let my emotions get the best of me." Blair finally admitted. "I saw that man walk in and all I could think about was grandma, and you and uncle Charlie, and Finley. I just felt this need to defend our farm and, jeez, Aunt Fran, I really gave it to that guy."

Fran had to smile at the innocence in her niece. She was brilliant, dedicated; but they often forgot how young she was because she was so mature for her age.

Getting up, Fran picked up her mug and walked around the table to Blair and wrapped a single arm around the beautiful young woman and whispered, "I wish I could have been there to see it. You're a wonderful, smart girl. You've done nothing wrong. And I bet you'll think of exactly the right thing to do – for the farm and for Finley. And knowing you, you'll look into it." Fran moved out of the room leaving Blair to sit with herself and the rest of the chai tea.

Look into it. That's exactly what she'd do. And, looking down at her afternoon cup of caffeine, she had just the fuel she needed to start now.

Santa Claus *ho-ho'd* as the last child walked out of the workshop grinning ear to ear with his parents. Christmas was only four days away, but he felt confident that the boy would wake up Christmas morning with exactly what he wished for.

Oh, how he loved when young children didn't wish for gifts that could be unwrapped, but gifts of love or generosity. His parents were in for a little surprise seeing as they thought they were finished having children, but they'd be just as elated as the young boy.

He watched them close the door and head toward the parking lot hand-in-hand.

Finley looked on, mesmerized. Unable to control her grin or her speculative mind, she folded her arms and leaned on the edge of his chair and asked, "Nick, are you the real Santa Claus?"

"Why of course I am!" His laugh jiggling his belly up and down. "I thought you figured that out a long time ago?"

Finley immediately thought back to her tenth Christmas and how she set out to learn once and for all if Santa Claus was real. She tilted her head at the memory and peered into Nick's eyes. He couldn't possibly be talking about *that*. How would he know? He couldn't.

A twinkle glistened in his eye and he winked at her stunned face.

"Now," he said, breaking her trance, "it looks like we have two days left, which is good." Nick spoke to Finley and to himself as he shrugged out of his red coat. "I have to get back to the Missus, and I have a very busy couple of days ahead of me."

Finley smirked, willing to play along, "The elves will wonder where you've been."

"Exactly," Nick agreed wholeheartedly.

"You know," Nick started again, "you haven't mentioned what it is you want for Christmas."

Finley grinned over the pain that was beginning to dull – for the time being. "I feel a little too old to wish for a gift from Santa Claus."

"Oh, no. Nobody is *ever* too old."

Reaching for the mop to clean the floors from their day of trampled snow and mud, Finley rested on the handle and closed her eyes, thinking of what she would wish for.

"I'd like to stop waiting on Christmas."

"I'm afraid I don't understand."

Finley rocked her resting chin to look at Nick. "Every year I feel as though I'm just waiting for Christmas to come. I'm hoping for something, someone, maybe a feeling. Then another year goes by and I find I'm disappointed. Then I wait again."

"Perhaps what you're waiting for isn't about Christmas as all?"

Finley thought about Jack and how he had made her feel so much joy in the short time they'd spent together. No, Finley agreed, maybe it wasn't about Christmas at all.

Then she thought about the kiss she received with a promise all those years ago. It wasn't so much Christmas, but the feeling of the kiss, the excitement of the promise, that had her holding out hope for so long. Ultimately letting her down. That's really what she wanted, she realized.

Still looking at Nick, Finley finally said, "I want a long-ago promise fulfilled." Smiling at her own nostalgia, she nodded. "I want what the promise meant. Love," she admitted. "I want the promise of love."

Nick's features softened into a smile, as if he finally heard from her what he was hoping to hear her entire life. "Ah, yes. That, my dear, is the most precious Christmas wish of all. And a very good one. Yes, yes. Very good."

Finley watched Nick turn to move toward the changing room as he bobbled his head up and down, still agreeing with Finley's wish.

How strange, she thought. Yes, very strange. But she couldn't help but feel a weight had lifted. She felt lighter. And as she began to clean, and a fresh sprinkle of snow started to fall just outside, Finley felt a little of the hope she'd lost all those years ago start to return.

CHAPTER 18

Jackson watched his brother, Jake slap a handful of papers onto a conference table that sat in between them all. It took every bit of self-control not to roll his eyes at the over-dramatic meltdown. He had enough warring around his mind, he didn't need his brother adding to the chaos.

"Care to explain yourself?" Jake spat the words in Jackson's direction.

"I could ask the same of you." Usually laid back, Jackson decided he'd had enough.

"Excuse me?" The surprise in Jake's voice didn't do much to hide the *how dare you challenge me* intent.

James sat and watched in silence, not daring to interrupt what was sure to be a battle. He'd sit it out until the subject of money dragged him in. Hopefully it wouldn't get to that point – at least not today, or right now, when both of his brother's thought it necessary to stand their ground.

Jackson stood and crossed the room, deciding to take his brother head on. "What were you even doing there? I emailed you an idea, exactly what you asked for. I didn't say it was a done deal."

"I needed to come and see for myself, it's what any good businessman would do."

"No, it's what a control-driven, untrustworthy associate would do."

Jackson held Jake's stare but could feel the wide-eyes of James looking on in surprise. He knew it because inside he couldn't believe he was making this much of a stand either.

"And thanks to you, we've lost more than a great opportunity. I lost something I love, *somebody* I love." Jackson turned on the thought of Finley and rubbed his hands down his face, then stopped and dropped his head. "Not that you would take two seconds to talk to me about anything other than business, or in this case, even that. You just need to run all over everything, be in charge. Just steamroll right through."

A long silence filled the room. Jake didn't know what to say any more than the other two. And Jackson had said his piece.

"Jackson, I–" Jake started after a moment, but was cut off.

"What that is," Jackson pointed to the paper spewed across the table, "is a great idea. It would have been ideal with Winter Haven, but if that doesn't work I'll find somebody else."

He walked to the door, stopping before he pulled the door open. "I'll see this project through, but after that, I'm done."

Then he walked out leaving his brothers gaping behind him.

Walking to his office, Jackson sat at his desk and stared at the file he'd put together that morning. If he couldn't talk to Finley, he'd try the next best thing when it came to farm operations – Blair. He wasn't sure how far he'd get with her, seeing as she didn't seem too keen on him taking a look at her projects. But this was good. *Really good.* And it deserved looking at, no matter how they were feeling right now.

Jackson took the next hour to read through all of its contents once more, then drafted an email to Blair and sent it off. Who knows if she'd get it that close to Christmas, but it was worth a shot.

Now all he needed to do was try and find a way to talk to Finley. He had walked away once, he wasn't about to do it again. At least not without her hearing him out.

Jackson picked up his coat from where he'd thrown it across the back of his chair and walked out, passing Jake and James on his way, without saying a word.

He had places to be.

With Christmas three days away, it was the last day the farm would be open before the grounds would empty and everything would quiet. Then they would enjoy holiday festivities of their own. At the end of the day, they would ceremoniously close the shops, the unpurchased trees would be hauled away and given as gifts to those who couldn't afford one, and the entire staff would gather for a Christmas dinner in the farmhouse. Dinner would be followed by dessert, drinks, and laughter. And the whole crew would stay late into the night, happily celebrating another successful season.

Finley couldn't help but snicker as she prepped the long dining table, and another brought up from storage, for the night's dinner. Her mother marched around the room disseminating orders to her father who was right at her heels, punching details into his phone.

"All of these candles should be lit. But I want them swapped out with the white ones at the top of the stairs by the basement. Think," Fran's hands spread wide in front of her as if she were illuminated, "bright, think starlight, think happy." Then she turned and kept moving.

Charlie stole a look at his daughter who could barely contain her laughter before he kicked up his feet and caught up with his wife as she started in on the sitting room.

Finley took stock of her own task. The long white runners spanned both of the tables and held the same white candles her dad would place on the mantel. Greenery and pinecones were scattered in between the tall tapers. There were enough placemats and table settings to accommodate the large crowd.

Eyeing the buffet that sat behind the table, Finley inhaled and took in the herby scent of turkey, savory stuffing, and what she knew to be the cheesy smell of scalloped potatoes. She'd have to head out for a bit when she was finished to keep from sampling the menu.

Maybe she'd take a walk up the hill. She'd put her good winter boots on, her outdoor hiking gear, and enjoy the winter day before joining everybody for a night of eating and drinking.

It didn't take her long to change or move into the wintry outdoors, though she did slow near the kitchen before thinking better of sneaking in for a quick taste. Finley inhaled the cool air and the welcome fresh feeling. Without waiting, she headed straight for the basin to start her climb.

Every now and then, Finley paused, looked down, and took in the farm. How had so much changed in the span of one winter season? She took a moment to sit on a tree stump and watch the movements below while she let her mind wander.

Not even four weeks ago she might have been willing to give the farm up. After deliberating on her guilt for a while, she decided she never would have gone through with the sale, though she would have seriously considered giving up ownership to another family member to pursue something new.

But after this season, seeing all of the good, the wonderful, and the beautiful; after feeling every bit a part of the farm and the happiness it brought others, there was no way she could leave now. She would miss it too much.

Finley let her eyes fall closed and thought of Jack. She had him to thank, in large part, for that realization. She began to see the farm through his eyes; the beauty, the gratifying hard work. And, she admitted, it was nice having somebody to enjoy it with. The early mornings, the cozy nights.

She missed him. She wasn't ashamed to admit it. He had made her laugh and get excited about her day. She looked forward to a moment spent with him, longed to see him when they weren't together, and when she had the chance to spot him from afar the feelings he stirred in her were like nothing she'd ever felt before.

Finley opened her eyes now. She had fallen for him. She had fallen in love with him.

And now he was gone. He had somehow maneuvered his way into her heart, but his true intentions had been somewhere else. It truly broke her heart. But she was glad to have been told the truth. Blair did what she herself would have done if anybody else would have been in her situation.

But she still missed him. Still loved him.

Finley lifted her hand to her cheek where he'd kissed it only days earlier.

Would somebody offer such a tender moment who didn't share her feelings of love?

She wondered. And thought about it more. What about the fire by the water's edge, the dancing, the early mornings, and the way when he looked at her it was as if he was seeing somebody he'd loved his whole life? That all had to mean something, didn't it?

Finley reached in her pockets and patted her gloved hands on the many zippered storage areas of her jacket – no phone.

She hopped up and made her way down the hill. She needed Maeve. Who better to talk to when she was in a moment of need. Maeve would give it to her straight, and hopefully tell her what she was thinking, and feeling, didn't make her a silly girl blinded by love.

"Maeve!" Finley shouted before she pushed all the way through the front door of the bakery.

Two elderly couples and a family of three stopped their conversations and lunches to stare.

Finely cringed and smiled awkwardly. "Sorry, here to see a friend about love. Everything's good. Everything's fine." She continued through the center of the room as the eyes followed her and she kept explaining. "Just hoping for a Christmas miracle. Have a great holiday."

When she disappeared into the kitchen she held the door closed behind her, grateful she was out of sight. But she found Miles standing wide-eyed before her, holding two doughy croissant rolls in his hands.

"Miles, I need–"

He held up both of the croissants and cut her off. "In the office." His head motioned to the back of the bakery.

Finely smiled. "Thanks." Then she ran.

"Maeve. Maeve."

The office, being the size of a cardboard box, didn't require the search party, but Finley couldn't hold in her excitement as she repeated her friend's name and took a seat while Maeve hung up from a call.

Finley leaned back at the arch in Maeve's brow and the grin and accompanied it.

"It's a girl."

"I know. I know, such a girl thing. But I – wait, what did you say?" Finley leaned forward again.

This time Maeve smiled bigger than Finley had ever seen and watched her friend's eyes fill. "It's a girl."

"Oh my gosh. Oh my gosh! It's a girl!" Finley flew out of her chair and swung around the small desk to wrap her friend in a hug and smother her with kisses. "It's a girl!"

The laughter was enough to carry through the kitchen and into the bakery where the guests couldn't help but smile at the sound coming from behind the walls. Miles just smiled and nodded as they looked up, happily questioning the commotion. What could he say? It was all he could do from bust out laughing with joy at learning his new baby was going to be daddy's sweet little girl.

Finley held and didn't let go. "I'm going to spoil her rotten. You can't stop me."

"I wouldn't dream of it. Now, I assume you didn't come in here kicking and screaming because you have telepathic tendencies."

"I didn't. But just give me another thirty seconds."

When Finley finally reclaimed her guest chair she said, "Okay, though in my mind I haven't moved on, I'm going to ask what I came to ask because the sooner I do the sooner I can swoon over a little unborn baby girl again."

"Yes," Maeve said, without hearing a question. "Because I believe in love, I believe in Jackson, and I'm extra mushy today."

"Wait, I didn't ask anything. I, did you say 'Jackson?'"

"I did." Maeve nodded.

"That's funny."

"What is?"

"That you'd think of Jackson, that boy from so long ago. What a strange slip. Your pregnancy must be getting to you already."

"Is it?" Maeve asked, leaning forward.

"Yes, well, yeah. Because I came to ask if you were me would you–"

"Yes."

"Will you let me finish?"

"I already know what you're going to ask. So, yes. Let Jackson be in love with you, and let yourself love him back. Everything else will work itself out."

Finley slouched and looked at Maeve, listening to her words. Then she whispered what Maeve had said aloud, "Let Jackson be in love with you."

Finley closed her eyes and remembered the kiss from years ago, and the other from only days earlier. One from a young boy named Jackson, and another from a man who had taken her heart, Jack. A man, she thought now as it came to her, who had captured her heart twice.

Her eyes flew open. "It's–"

177

"Yes. Yes, it is." Maeve nodded.

Finley mirrored her friends nod, though much more enthusiastically. Then quietly stood and slowly walked out of the office.

Needing a walk of her own, Blair stretched as she moved out the back door and stood, wondering where she should go. As she turned the corner to head toward the stables where Trish and Carl would be cleaning for the day and pampering the horses that would be spoiled with a brush, treats, and well-deserved rest.

"Oh, hello," Blair said, as she nearly ran into a stocky looking man that looked like he was heading into their office. "Can I help you, sir?"

The man stopped short of knocking on the door at Blair's question. "Hello, perhaps you can. I'm here to see Finley Whittaker. I'd like to follow up on some business with her, to see if she's given any thought to a proposal of mine."

Blair stared at the man as the blood rushed from her head and the recognition of a huge mistake was settling in.

"Ah, she's out just now. I'm the farm's operational manager, Blair Whittaker, is there something I can help you with?"

The man beamed and offered a jovial hand, "Well, you just might. My name is Connor Jorgenson. I haven't heard back from Ms. Whittaker regarding an offer of purchase, and I was hoping to sit with her to see if I could help answer questions, and quite frankly, try and sway her."

Blair gulped, confirming one final detail for herself. "You don't happen to know a Jack Bloom, do you?"

This time Mr. Jorgenson gave a questioning look, then shook his head. "I can't say that I do. Should I?"

"No. No you shouldn't." Deciding to approach this conversation a bit differently than she did that last on the topic of buying the property, Blair smiled. "I apologize, Mr. Jorgenson. I'm happy to take a card from you. But I believe the family has decided not to sell at this time. Though, I can assure you, if we have your contact information and we ever agree as a unit it's time to sell, we'll keep you in mind."

Blair watched Connor Jorgenson slowly take in the view of the farm, turning in a slow circle. When he finally made it all the way around he grinned and gave a single nod.

"I can't blame you for making the decision. It's quite a sight; it's quite a place." He offered another hand to part amicably and said, "Thank you for keeping me in mind."

Before he disappeared around the farmhouse, curiosity got the better of her. Blair asked, "Mr. Jorgenson?"

"Yes?" He paused, turning toward her.

"Can I ask what has you so interested in this property?"

Now a warm smile came to his face, followed by a bit of rose-color in his cheeks. "Of course. It's where I proposed to my wife thirty years ago."

Blair didn't know what to say, so she said nothing. Just offered a warm smile and a dip of her head, then watched him disappear.

CHAPTER 19

Finley tried Jackson on his phone to no avail.

So, this is what that feels like.

She thought about all the calls she let roll to voicemail, unable to deal with the heartbreak of hearing his voice. Now on the other end she realized the anticipation of not knowing if the other will answer, only to have them not, was agonizing.

Staring at her reflection, Finley decided she would do what she needed to in the morning. Tonight, was a night for celebrating. They had another amazing year on the farm. Sales were the highest they've ever been, the staff had a certain energy about them she hadn't seen in years, and the biggest excitement of all was upon them: Christmas Eve and Christmas Day were nearly here.

Finley imagined getting up early, ready to spend the festive holiday with her family. There would be food, drinks, movies, football on TV, then a game to follow in the snow lit only by the farm lights outside. They would exchange presents, have eggnog by the fireside, share stories from the year, then eagerly head to bed.

Grinning at the thought, Finley thought of Christmas Day. How no matter how old they all got, there was always a present from Santa Claus waiting for them beneath the tree. They'd gather in their pajamas and robes, feet in slippers, and coffee in hand. They would take their place around the Christmas tree that would stay lit throughout the night, and one-by-one open their single gift.

She hoped everybody could celebrate like they did, or in just a way that gave them the same sense of happiness, family, familiarity, and beauty.

Leaving her phone behind, Finley finally made her way down the stairs toward the voices that were already echoing through the halls.

Blair had tried to track Finley down all day, finally giving up when she decided it was either: scour the grounds and show up to the party a wreck, or enjoy the process of getting dressed up for the holiday party and wait to see Finley there.

She made one last stop at the office to double check once more there weren't any loose ends going into the holiday before she'd take the next two days off – completely detaching from work.

Sliding into her chair, Blair pulled up her to-do list and noted there wasn't a single line unchecked. Then she clicked open her email and scanned for anything urgent.

Her gasp was audible when she came across the last email.

Subject: Project Proposal. From: Bloom, Jackson.

After twenty-five minutes of skimming the file she found attached to the email, Blair leaned back in her chair and arched her brows to match the surprise in her eyes. Jack – or *Jackson,* she corrected herself as she saw how he'd signed his email with his full name – had covered every detail of her project from his company's perspective. Down to the map of where their trees and products would sit in his company's parking lots. Amazing.

This was the type of company she was looking for. And – *oh my God* – after how she'd treated him she couldn't believe he'd even taken the time to reach out.

Blair covered her face and moaned at her terrible mix-up. *But,* she thought again, *he still took the time to reach out.*

This couldn't be just about the farm. She leaned forward and tried to read between the professional lines. She read words like 'rustic berry wreaths' and 'delicious Christmas cookies.' Scrolling up she saw the way he described the 'full and magnificent trees' that would be 'perfect for their clientele.' Reading more, she saw more than a simple proposal.

It meant more to him than business.

Blair smiled.

He loved the farm. *And,* she thought, *he loved more than just the farm.*

Flexing and wriggling her fingers, Blair quickly found the keys of her laptop and hit reply. Grinning her way through her plan, she signed off leaving her number and sent up a quick little Christmas wish that everything would work out.

Then she closed her laptop and decided there was nothing left to do now but wait and celebrate the best holiday with her closest friends and family.

Laughter, singing, and loud voices sang throughout the farmhouse as everybody feasted. They all took turns sharing stories of Christmases past and new memories from this year on the farm.

As Finley looked down the long table, the candles burning low, spirits riding high, she knew there was nowhere in the world she'd rather be. It seemed so cliché to think something like that, but it was true.

Reading her mind, Blair reached over and took her hand and gave it a little squeeze. They had something wonderful. Truly magical.

"Why don't you leave the dishes to me this year," Blair said as she followed Finley into the kitchen.

"We don't even do them, we just shove them into the dishwasher, I can help."

"What if I told you I had an ulterior motive?"

Finley shook her head and smirked at the young woman's wiggling eyebrows. "Fine, what's the trade off?"

"I know there's no work tonight, but there's something I really want you to see. But," Blair urged, "I don't want you to be distracted.

Maybe you could take what I give you and head outside for some quiet and consideration. And just, well, really think about it."

Squinting suspiciously at Blair, Finley hesitated before she finally agreed. "Okay, if you think now is the best time."

"I do." Blair tried not to let the words fly out too quickly, though she knew she was failing miserably. "I do," she said again, more collected and calmer. "It would mean a lot to me."

That was the dagger. Though Blair knew she had her on the hook, Finley wouldn't be able to deny something that was personal to her.

"Okay, what do you want me to look at?"

"It's in the folder on your desk. Take your time, but when you're ready, you know, let me know."

"Yeah, yeah. Okay, I'm going."

As soon as Finley was out of sight, Blair reached for her phone and quickly sent out a message.

"What kind of a plan are you working in here?" Fran moved in once she could get Blair alone. She'd watched the exchange and knew something was up, but didn't want to disrupt a plan in motion. She had a feeling, and she rarely argued with feelings.

"Ah," Blair let her mouth hang open, "nothing. It's nothing."

"It doesn't look like nothing."

Looking to the door and back to Fran, she moved in and stood face-to-face with her aunt. Her plan spewed out in record time.

All Fran could do was stare. She knew the name Jack from the man her daughter had fallen in love with, and from the heartbreak he caused when he left.

But she also knew the name Jackson, and when she heard it she had another feeling. Could it really be who her daughter spent years as an innocent child talking about and wondering if he would return? Every year she saw a little hope dim in her precious daughters' eyes, but it never left, not all the way.

"Well," Fran said, "we'll have to see what happens." Fran watched Blair question herself for a moment at the response. Then she added, "But I have a good feeling."

Jackson sat at the coffee shop, staring at his phone, waiting for what seemed like eternity. He told himself Blair would come through, he just had to trust her. He couldn't believe the chain of events that had gotten him to this point, but after she explained everything he supposed it made a little sense. And he did get a good laugh out of her mistaking his brother for the slick suited man who tried to swoop in and buy the farm. Though, he had to admit, he couldn't blame the guy for trying.

When his phone finally buzzed, he fumbled it before grabbing hold and reading the message.

It was time.

Grabbing his coat and leaving a tip on the table, he quickly tried to make it to the door. When he reached it, he couldn't believe who was walking in.

"Why, Jackson!" Nick exclaimed, "What a pleasant surprise. What brings you out to the coffee shop tonight?"

"Nick, so great to see you. I'm actually just heading out, in a bit of a hurry. I was waiting for a message," he lifted his phone as evidence, "and it just came in."

"Oh, sure, sure. You know," Nick said, his rosy cheeks plumping in a smile, "I wonder if you would give this card to Finley when you see her. I meant to give it to her, but by-gosh, I completely forgot."

"Of course, I–" Jackson looked down and read Finley's name in ornate script writing and looked up. He hadn't told Nick he was going to Winter Haven. But Nick only stared back with twinkling eyes. "Yes, of course. I'll make sure she gets it."

"I knew I could count on you."

Jackson heard Nick's words and somehow felt they meant more than for the simple act of delivering a card. Though he ignored it, something inside of him agreed with the jovial man.

"I should," Jackson pointed to the door, "probably get going."

"Now's the perfect time. Oh, and Jackson?"

"Yeah?" Jackson said, as he slowed and turned after putting his hands in his jacket pockets, covering them from the snow that began to fall around him.

"Merry Christmas."

Jackson grinned and replied, "Merry Christmas to you too, Santa."

Finley moved out into the cold just as the snow began to fall. Unable to control the joyful feeling it gave her, she leaned her head back and let the flakes find her warm face.

She wandered for a bit before she realized she had arrived at the old hay bale sitting outside of Santa's workshop.

"How fitting," she said to herself. If there was any better place for her to sit to make an important decision, she didn't know of it.

Crossing her feet beneath her, Finley sat for a moment before opening the folder to look at the first page. She stared for another minute, glancing at the words but not reading them. Instead she noticed the neat file with little note tabs marked on the side with Blair's detailed comments. Then she got distracted by the intricate flakes that fell to the paper and melted, leaving little gray speckles of damp behind.

Without reading a word, she closed the file and let her gloved hand rest on top. She didn't need to read the file in detail. She would, eventually. But if Blair thought this was it, then it was. It was time Blair was given the trust, and the credit she deserved.

What a change this would be for the farm. It would be more work, but it would be exciting.

Looking back toward the farmhouse she took in the golden light shining from every window and watched everybody moving in and out of the window frames, talking, sipping drinks, and laughing. No more business, she wanted to go in and join the festivities.

Standing, Finley brushed off her jeans, and clumsily knocked the file to the ground and watched the papers spill out.

"Of course," Finely said, laughing to herself.

"Somebody is going to have to teach you how to stay on top of that thing."

With her hands and knees on the snowy ground, Finley looked up. She heard the familiar, wonderful voice, but she couldn't quite believe he was there.

Jackson moved to her, then crouched slowly, helping her pick up the strewn papers. He recognized the document the moment he saw it but said nothing, just kept his eyes locked on hers. With the file put back together, Jackson took Finley's hand and helped her to her feet.

"You're here." Finley finally said, not knowing what else to say, since her head and her heart were so happy to see him, but she didn't know how to start.

Rather than speak, Jackson leaned in, still holding her hand, and let his lips linger on her cheek. He breathed her in and let the warmth move between them.

When he moved back ever so slightly, Finley's eyes were closed and a stray tear slipped down her cheek.

"It's you," she whispered, finally opening her eyes.

"I promised I would come back."

Laughing through a happy cry, Finley smiled and let Jackson wipe the tear.

"It's about time," she started, then her eyes focused as she playfully said, "but I'm not selling you the farm."

It was Jackson's turn to share her humor. "I don't want it."

Finley stepped back only slightly, "What? But I thought–"

Jackson only shook his head. "I do love the farm, I always have. Ever since that day we were ten years old." He closed the small gap between them. "But, there's something I love more. And I dreamed of her for twenty years."

Shamelessly wanting to hear him say it, Finley asked, "And that is?"

"I love this farm," he began to lean in to kiss her, "but I'm in love with you."

As soon as he said the words her arms flung around him and she pressed her lips to his.

They stood, arms wrapped tightly around each other, not wanting to let go, until they heard the knocks on the windows and the shouting and cheering coming from inside the farmhouse. When they realized they were being watched, their shy laughter at being caught was shared, but neither of them minded.

Finley kept her hands linked behind Jacksons neck and lifted her head to look at him. "Make me another promise?" she asked.

"Anything."

"Promise you'll stay for Christmas?"

This time Jackson grinned and nodded, then said, "And every Christmas after."

Not wanting the moment to end, Finley felt Jackson slowly pull away, but she supposed they couldn't stand out in the cold kissing and hugging all night. Eventually they'd have to make their way inside. And, if she was being honest with herself, she couldn't wait to join the party with Jackson by her side. But when he moved only a little she looked down and watched him reach into his pocket.

"I was told to give you this." He pulled out the card Nick had given him only minutes earlier.

Finely looked at the card, then to Jackson, confused. She took it, slid off her glove, and began to open it. When she took a moment to glance at Jackson he only shrugged, not knowing what she'd find inside.

She pulled out a card with beautiful script writing on it and read:

Dearest Finley,

I've been waiting years to be able to deliver this card to you. And now it's time.

A promise is something to be cherished, and is precious when kept. Sometimes they can be hard to keep, but when two people are ready, what magic a promise can bring.

I'm hoping you can make a promise to me. Promise me you'll stop waiting on Christmas, or a promise, or love. You're ready.

Always,

Mr. C

Finley looked up in surprise.

"What is it?" Jackson asked.

Thinking about what the note said, she smiled and shook her head. "Nothing, it's nothing at all."

Feeling as though he understood, he held out his hand and made a slight turn toward the farmhouse. "Are you ready?" he asked.

Laughing at his choice of words, and meaning so much more than what her simple response offered, she smiled and said, "I'm ready."

Jackson kissed Finley's cheek once more, then they walked hand-in-hand through the falling snow, knowing they'd finally made the most important promise of all – a promise of love.

THANK YOU!

I'm so humbled that you've taken the time to read my book. I can't tell you how much of my heart goes into each and every word.

I WOULD BE SO GRATEFUL FOR YOUR HONEST REVIEW OF:
WAITING ON CHRISTMAS

Scan the QR code below to be taken to Amazon.
(Hover your phone over the image!)

ARE YOU READY FOR MORE?

Keep flipping pages for:

A MAGICAL NEW RELEASE

TWO NEW SWEET HOLIDAY ROMANCE BOOKS

AN EXCLUSIVE LOOK AT *Postmark Christmas*

THE PROBLEM WITH *love* POTIONS

A LANTERN LANE ROM COM

A ROMANTIC COMEDY

KATIE BACHAND

THE PROBLEM WITH LOVE POTIONS

The Problem with Love Potions is a laugh-out-lough, seasonal rom com about a half-hazard witch who tries to make her reluctant soulmate fall in love with her. Its sweet, so fun, and will leave you smiling from start to finish!

Scan below for the Amazon Sales Page
(Hover your phone over the image!)

NEW HOLIDAY ROMANCE

KATIE
BACHAND

A BORROWED CHRISTMAS LOVE STORY

A Borrowed Christmas Love Story is a sweet, Hallmark-style holiday romance that thrusts two people into the unknown love stories of their grandparents. Perhaps both were too quick to judge their grandparents' decision to remarry so late in life. And perhaps the love story they learn about isn't unlike their own.

Scan below for the Amazon Sales Page
(Hover your phone over the image!)

NEW HOLIDAY ROM COM

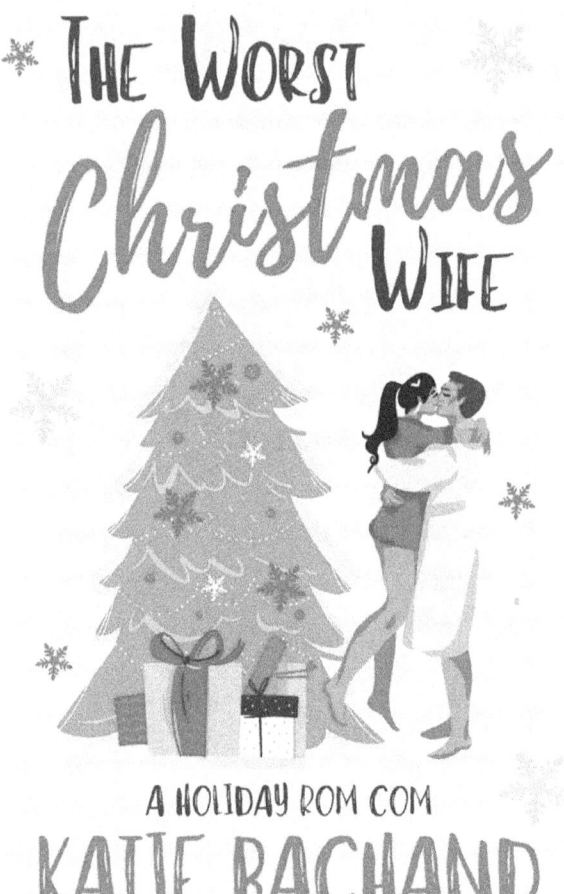

The Worst Christmas Wife

A HOLIDAY ROM COM
KATIE BACHAND

THE WORST CHRISTMAS WIFE

The Worst Christmas Wife is a laugh-out-lough, holiday rom com about one (extremely handsome) grumpy boss that needs a wife, one over-qualified new assistant that needs a raise and a promotion, and two attracted-to-each-other people who hate that they need each other to make it happen.

Scan below for the Amazon Sales Page
(Hover your phone over the image!)

START READING

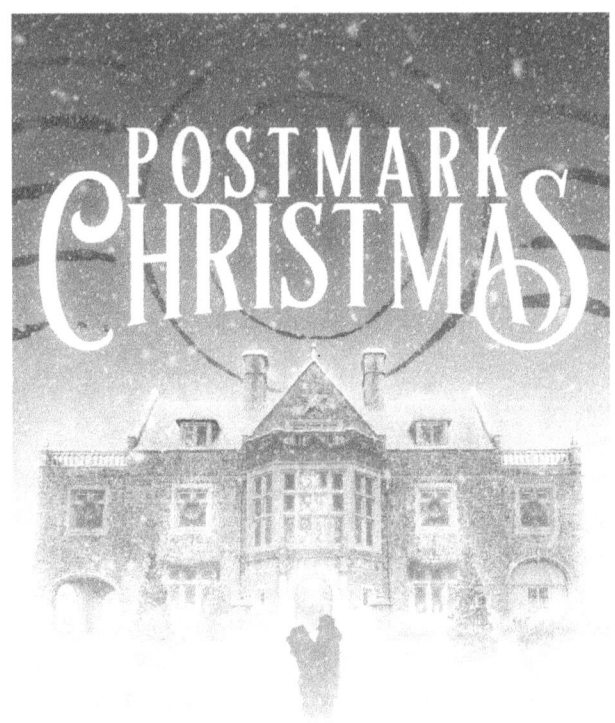

KATIE
BACHAND

CHAPTER 1

Harlow Hill had been listening to Christmas music since July. She told herself it was because of the job. Her clients started putting together holiday commercials, print advertisements, and plans for their festive – and usually over-the-top – holiday parties even before their Independence Day events were over.

But she knew, even without the big-ticket clients and events, she would still be yearning for Christmas. She would be sneaking in a holiday music session while working out, or turning the air conditioning up at The Hill – her inherited Victorian mansion on Summit Avenue – and throwing on some cozy winter pajamas, opening a bottle of eggnog, and settling in for the Hallmark Channel's *Christmas in July* event.

Thank God somebody out there had the right mind to air adorable, romantic Christmas movies when the temperature outside was ninety-eight and the air so humid your glasses would fog up just moving from inside to out.

Sally, who was preparing to give her weekly project update, was just as excited about it as Harlow. Though she was usually a little less restrained and reserved in her presentation.

"Hi! Good morning! Are you ready for our update?" Sally asked as she bounded into Harlow's office, her words a mixture of singing and shouting.

Sally, Harlow noted upon her entrance, was wearing the same winter white color of the walls and the same red accent. Only instead of concrete, her sweater was a chunky knit, and instead of red picture frames and vases, her earrings and necklace were a mixture of berry-red beads and feathers.

Harlow couldn't help but smile at the enthusiastic young woman. Sally wasn't unlike Harlow had been as a young marketing and advertising executive. Maybe that's why she'd always had a soft spot for the vibrant, and ambitious brunette.

"I am absolutely ready. Come in. Who else is joining today?" Harlow gestured to the leather chesterfield sofa across from her desk, and Sally sat.

Harlow knew Sally wouldn't need any of the staff to help in the breakdown of every excruciating and finite detail of their plans, but Sally – and Harlow too, admittedly – loved having the room filled and hearing from the team as they recounted the status of the projects they owned. All of them were competitive, but overwhelmingly supportive.

"We'll have Ryan and Vanessa. Jacquelyn is on-site setting up for her skating event this weekend. Which, if I might add, is amazing." Sally said, while her hazel eyes grew two sizes, letting a dreamy haze cloud across them as she looked off into the distance. "Her decision to go with *A Log Cabin Christmas* theme was dead-on. The evergreens she brought in are the perfect pine green, and they are adorned with these chunky amber lights, fragrant cinnamon pinecones, red robin ornaments, and the presents are wrapped in buffalo-check paper. Seriously, it's like walking into an LL Bean catalog."

"Oh my God, are you talking about *A Log Cabin Christmas?*" Vanessa asked, catching the last couple words while running through the door. Attempting to be on time once this week, and to not spill her coffee upon entry. "It is glorious and rugged perfection. It makes me want to live in a cabin and dress in plaid."

Vanessa plopped next to Sally on the chesterfield as Ryan sauntered in, completely cool and unfazed that he was five minutes late. He took one of the wooden chairs that bordered the couch, sliding effortlessly in and offering a killer smile.

Oh the hearts he would break, Harlow thought, and the pining hearts he was creating. Sally, the ever put-together professional, had to force herself to concentrate just a bit more when Ryan walked in.

Harlow watched the three sit expectantly, and loved everything about them. All so different, but all of them beautiful, passionate, and driven.

She'd heard friends and colleagues from other companies tell her that millennials were lazy and ruining their corporate drive. Harlow had seen first-hand that was far from true. She'd never seen individuals have so much fun and try so hard to produce results in her lifetime. They embraced the old, and she loved that they understood and drove them toward the new.

"Okay," Harlow began, "let's get started. It sounds like Jacquelyn is on track. Is there anything she needs from me that wasn't in her recap email this morning? Does she need any assistance in set-up or opening?"

"She is on top of it." Sally took the lead. "All decorations are in place. Props – like the wooden toboggan sleds and the hay bales for on-ice seating – arrived yesterday. Those should be in place by," Sally looked at her watch, more out of habit than a need to see it was ten after nine, "now."

Sally drew her chestnut hair over one shoulder, not realizing her nervous habit, and went on. "The food vendors are scheduled to arrive at five tomorrow morning. They are expecting a crowd. At least double what they had last year since it was such a hit. And it's the Saturday before Thanksgiving so it's anticipated that a lot of people won't be working next week. Jacq calculated for that, too."

"Perfect. Please let me know if you hear of anything from her. I know she'll reach out to one of you before me, but I'm available." Harlow nodded, took a sip of her coffee, and made a note that everything was on track. "Okay, Vanessa, how are you doing at the hotel?"

"Good. We are back on track after the delivery mix-up last week."

Harlow appreciated Vanessa's word choice. 'Mix-up,' to Harlow's mind, was putting it extremely nicely. The florist sent less than half of the greenery, garland, and poinsettia order. And what they did send went to the wrong hotel – in the wrong state. Apparently, Minnesota and Michigan were easily interchangeable.

Vanessa had simply gotten on the phone, redirected the shipment, got a refund for the undelivered items, covered the charge for the delivery, worked with a local flower and garden shop, and had the rest of the delivery the following Monday.

"I've confirmed with Sasha – the hotel's event planner – the room will be set up by tomorrow morning. We're talking over-the-top blues and silvers – on and in everything. Bulbs, flowers, tassels, vases, and even the food. The caterer is prepared and we've confirmed the headcount. Entertainment was set up last night and they'll arrive by three tomorrow. That's four hours before the seven o'clock start time. And their equipment – silver."

Vanessa looked around and saw her comment received smiles from the room. They knew it was ridiculous too, but it was just the right amount of obnoxious.

"Hors d'oeuvres will be served to the five hundred guests upon arrival – cute, dainty finger-foods. There will be holiday cocktails, beer, and wine available for beverages straight through the night. A plated dinner will be served at eight with light holiday music continuing to play in the background. At nine the dessert bar will be set up. The Bistro will provide the treats and do set up and break down. I've seen the spread – they look delectable. And if any of you make it, they are making extra dinner plates for emergencies, it's roasted rack of lamb with blueberry glaze." Vanessa moaned as she pretended to faint falling to the tufted back-rest. "There are no words."

"Music will pick up at that point, offering a more festive beat." Vanessa sat up and went on. "It will hopefully encourage dancing *and* for those in attendance to open their wallets. There is a raffle for prizes large and small. All proceeds going to Heritage House. It's an orphanage in downtown St. Paul."

Heartfelt *ahh's* made their way out of Sally and Ryan at the generous gesture.

Vanessa agreed and went on to tell the group it was the first party thrown by two accounting firms that joined forces in October. There were good feelings all around and she couldn't wait to celebrate with them – they'd invited her as a guest to her own party.

Ryan then lived his own bit of excitement as he recounted the details of his event taking place at the NHL hockey arena in St. Paul. It was all-man, or all-fan, appropriate.

Miniature hockey gear ornaments took over the trees that would be lit up all around the rink and near the concessions areas on every floor. Over four-hundred of them. Minnesota's team had donated signed jerseys, posters, sticks, and pucks to the event.

"Everything is good. The only thing I might need help with is the final walk-through for the charity executives. They are hoping for a picture at the opening of everybody who came together to make the event happen. Harlow, are you available for that?"

"Friday, December 13th?" Harlow asked, mostly for Ryan's sake, to let him dictate, but she knew their schedules inside and out.

"Nailed it. Could you be there around six?"

"Perfect."

Ryan smiled proudly, and Sally and Vanessa nodded at themselves for an update well done. Their pride lasted until Lisa, the busiest one of them all, ran into the room.

"Did I miss it? I missed it. Shit." Lisa asked and answered her own question, then plopped herself on the chair across from Ryan, and sank in exhaustion.

Harlow, and the rest, attempted to hide their amusement as they watched the new mom chug coffee like she would water after running a marathon through the snow. And by the look of her boots that hadn't yet been changed into heels, she might have done just that.

"I'll give you the update. Everybody is executing perfectly." Harlow sent appreciative and proud looks toward the group then continued, "We are on track and it seems it's going to be a very Merry Christmas."

"Thank God. What is Christmas again?" Lisa joked as she looked up, pretending to be confused, then added, "I'll meet up with each of you in our one-on-ones to make sure there isn't anything else you need from me, or last-minute details you'd like my help with."

"Sounds great, Lis." Ryan said, the first to get up and walk out with a wave, then he answered a phone call from one of his clients he greeted by name.

"Lisa, you're stunning. Even in your frazzled, no-sleep, new baby world. It's making you sparkle like a fresh, fluffy snow," Sally said as she followed Ryan out and tapped Vanessa on the shoulder, a sign that told her she should follow suit.

Vanessa stood, reached over to squeeze Lisa's hand, winked, and followed Sally. The women walked out organizing a trip to a coffee shop for their next meeting. And they'd need it seeing as they'd be putting in a long couple of weeks, and many days with hours that would reach well into double digits.

Harlow looked at Lisa and smiled sympathetically but with as much joy she knew Lisa's new baby brought into the world.

"How is sweet baby Layla?" Harlow asked.

"She's great. The most precious, unsleeping human on the planet."

"What if you just took a couple more weeks off. I promise we will be fine here." Harlow didn't have the heart to tell Lisa that when she was gone things trudged forward, but barely.

It was hard losing the one person who knew everybody's schedule; scheduled all the meetings, job interviews, client interviews; had relationships with the event planners from the hotels, local, and national caterers; knew where to get the best deals, and understood the ins and outs of tailoring your mood and correspondence to appeal to the right people for the right occasions.

"Not a chance. I need a break. Even if it is so I can sleep at my desk. But if it gets to that point, I promise I'll book one of the mother rooms. Might as well hook myself up to the pump if I'm going to be still for more than ten minutes," Lisa said, pointing to her boobs like they were feeding objects rather than an appreciated and appealing part of her body.

"Okay, but if it gets to be too much, you tell me. Before we get too into work, what can I bring for Thanksgiving?" Harlow asked, excited about the holiday that was now only six days away.

"Yourself and your favorite bottle of wine. Nothing more, nothing less. You know how Mom and Steve get. They rule the kitchen and no outsider must enter."

Lisa and Harlow both understood the term 'outsider' was affectionately used for any person who wasn't her mom or her doting husband, which included family.

"Understood." Harlow saluted.

"Did you call them?" Lisa asked, changing the subject, knowing Harlow's family had been on her mind.

Harlow thought of them constantly, but more so around the holidays. Lisa knew the Hills came from money. She'd known since she and Harlow were childhood friends going to the same elementary and high schools. But as people do, they had drifted apart during college and the first couple of years back in St. Paul. It wasn't until Lisa had applied for the Executive Event Coordinator job that they had reconnected. They'd hit it off again immediately and filled a void in each other's lives they hadn't realized was missing.

When they rekindled their old friendship, Harlow had confided in Lisa that the money was still there, but the once-close family had begun to jet-set around the world and hopping around to live in different states. Vincent, Harlow's brother, had moved his wife, Catherine, to New York to open a branch of their marketing and advertising company there. And Harriett, her sister, had done the same but had taken her skills to Nashville. Her parents, Walter and Vivienne, had since retired and liked to spend the holidays in France, Italy, or any other picturesque European country.

This year, Harlow had waffled and wavered on reaching out to them to see if they'd all come home for Christmas to spend it together like they used to.

"I haven't." Harlow's head dropped, showing disappointment in herself and readied for a stern talking-to from Lisa.

Lisa got up and sat on the coffee table so she could sit and reach across Harlow's desk to take her hand.

"I promise it won't be hard. Just a quick call. Or even a text. Just send a quick feeler out there to get everybody's schedules?"

"It's not the schedules I'm worried about. And calling or texting isn't the hard part. It's the answer that I might get in response. I'm afraid to hear they won't be able to make it. Or, that they offer I go to them – which would be really nice – but it's not home." Harlow shook her head.

"I know. I understand," Lisa said, letting out a sigh for her friend. She understood, because even though her parents and extended family were always around and she had them for all holidays and special occasions, she couldn't imagine how sad she would be if one day she didn't have that. "But promise me you'll keep thinking about it. Your family is wonderful. I bet they just don't realize how much you all would love it. How much you all need it."

"I promise. Lis, you are amazing. And you do actually 'sparkle like freshly fallen snow.'"

The women laughed at Sally's description from the meeting, but only out of appreciation. And, if Harlow wasn't mistaken in her friend's glow, it was the truth.

CHAPTER 2

"Thanks, Brandon. Yeah, if you could have that ready by the time I get up that would be great. We aren't wasting any time on this."

Harris Porter stomped his boots, shook out his tailored winter coat, and tenderly smoothed and brushed the flakes out of his styled hair upon walking into the building.

He continued to listen to Brandon, his number one product manager, confirm he'd be able to have information ready on the feed company they were looking to collaborate with by the time he made it up to their offices.

Hopefully the collaboration he was working on would happen in the *very* near future. Very near if he could convince – probably more like beg – his dad. Maybe by the second quarter if he pressed hard. And fourth quarter if he let it happen organically and didn't come up against any hurdles along the way.

"Perfect. Just walked in. Be up in five," Harris said, before he swung the second set of doors open that led to the completely modernized Creamery, Co.

Harris looked around and smiled at the angled, black strips of wood that paneled the reception desk, noting it looked modern but balanced out the white walls and the concrete desk tops, floors, and pillars. It was a remodel his dad had let him take on only a couple years earlier. Now, it matched their website and appealed to the younger generation – who were going to be their new customer and employee demographic.

He grinned but was baffled by the thought that the 'younger generation' no longer included himself. There was an entire youthful generation coming up behind him. They were ready to work, and ready for their work to make the world a better place. That's why this feed collaboration was so critical to their success.

Yes, he thought, he'd use that in his pitch to his dad. Charles Porter had made his own father's creamery business into a billion-dollar company. Harris had helped Charles turn it into a multi-billion-dollar company. And there was so much more they could do.

Harris jumped at the clank that sounded from behind him. When he turned he saw two boxes, at least six-feet-tall, trying to cram through the oversized double doors.

"Wait, wait!"

Harris whirled around once more to see Nancy Lawson, their front desk receptionist yell, while waving her hands to try and halt the delivery man.

"Good morning, Harris. How are you today?" Nancy asked as she whooshed by.

"Great," Harris responded quickly, hoping to get it in before she was out of earshot. "How are you?" he asked, letting out a smirk knowing she was too nice not to keep the conversation going.

"Oh, really," Nancy huffed, "really great." She turned her head slightly and lifted her voice. "The kids and grandkids all made it in last night."

Nancy huffed out another couple of breaths as she and the delivery man continued to reach opposite sides of the box in their repeated attempt to find each other.

"Can you imagine, ten adults and seven kids, all under the same roof? For a month. More actually. They are staying until the New Year." She shook her head stopped her tilting and put up a finger in Harris' direction, showing she'd be right back with him.

"Sir," Nancy greeted the driver after hovering on one side long enough to finally catch him, "good morning to you. I hope you are doing very well. You are soaked to the bone. We'll have to get you some coffee or a hot chocolate. But before then," she continued without letting the driver respond – and he seemed okay with that as long as he got the hot chocolate, as that's when his eyes and eyebrows perked – "you'll have to take this back outside. We have a delivery entrance and it will be much easier for you there. I promise. No squeezing through doors or scuffing my floors. Once you have it in, you come find me, and I'll have a hot cup waiting for you."

"Yes ma'am." The young driver nodded, gave a little salute, and was pulling the gigantic boxes back out the small opening he tried to jam them through.

Nancy turned on a dime and Harris watched the fit grandmother of seven speed walk back to her throne.

"Nicely done." Harris said, genuinely impressed.

Nancy nodded firmly, but added a smile that let Harris know she was back to their original conversation.

"What are you all doing for the holidays?"

"I'm probably working straight through. We've got some big opportunities knocking on our door." Harris wasn't lying about either, there was a good chance he'd miss the holidays this year.

"Harris." Nancy's motherly tone sounded like his own mom's disapproval of his working habits. "You have to make time for the holidays *and* for family. It's what's most important."

"I am – I will," Harris agreed, but his agreement wasn't as truthful, "But this is setting us up for the future. We will never have a want in the world. And, we'll be helping a lot of people."

Nancy looked at Harris. He was the same age as her youngest son, and she adored him just as much. She, like Harris she supposed, remembered a time when his father, Charles, had been frugal and unwilling to spend any of their hard-earned money. Charles hadn't been much different than Harris himself. As a result, they'd grown up humbly. It wasn't a bad thing, but she imagined Harris had felt the impact and never wanted to say he couldn't afford something. Whenever she pressed, it was always 'one more deal' or 'one more sale or collaboration," *Then* there would be enough. *Then* he would settle down.

She wished she could shake some sense into him.

"As long as you promise to at least take the important days off. Thanksgiving, Christmas Eve, and Christmas day. If for no other reason than realizing that you won't have anybody to work with." Nancy smiled at the laugh she got out of Harris. "You have very kindly given the company twelve holidays and those are three of them. Four if you include the day after Thanksgiving – so you might as well add that to your list too."

"I'll do my best," Harris agreed. It was genuine, and it was true that he'd be hard pressed to reach anybody on those days. He'd think about it more seriously since she brought up that point. And, if he showed up to the holidays it would make his mom happy – and maybe make his dad loosen up to the feed collaboration idea.

"Hey Nance," Harris said, his curiosity getting the best of him, "what was in those boxes?"

"Oh, one of them was a big tree and as many lights and ornaments we could fit into the empty spaces. The other was a giant post box for your dad's *Postmark Christmas* campaign. It's so wonderful, that idea."

"Don't we have at least twenty other trees in storage?"

Without missing a beat and without giving the chance for him to argue, Nancy looked Harris in the eye and smiled sweetly, "Now, we have twenty-one."

Harris laughed and nodded, accepted that apparently one office building could never have too many Christmas trees, then waved and headed to the elevator to make his way to the top floor. A floor, he had noted earlier that morning, that was already decorated, and exploding with Christmas reds and greens.

CHAPTER 3

Snow had been scarce in early November, but the cool flakes that fell now warmed Harlow's heart as she watched them fall while rocking Layla in her second-floor nursery.

Lisa and Steve had decorated it with plush blankets, fuzzy animals in whites, tans, and browns, and soft gauzy curtains that were just the right amount of precious baby-girl. The delicate chimes of a *Baby's First Christmas* snow globe were already filling the sweet little room. Some things just couldn't wait, Harlow thought, as she closed her eyes and listened as Layla slept in her arms.

When the music stopped Harlow looked down and envied the peacefulness of the darling face as she slept. She could have put Layla down minutes ago but the feeling of holding the sleeping baby tugged at her heart and amplified her longing to love. So she would love, hold, and rock this borrowed baby even if only for another ten minutes.

When Harlow had finally separated herself from Layla she stepped out and stretched, thankful she'd decided on an oversized sweater for the day. She'd eaten more in that one Thanksgiving meal than she typically did in a week. She vowed to never eat again as she pushed away from the table earlier. And wouldn't you know it, she was almost ready to go back for round two.

"If you're thinking what I think you're thinking, you go first, because then I won't feel as guilty."

Harlow laughed at Lisa's ability to read her mind and nodded as though she'd been caught.

"I can't help it. It was too good. I was actually wondering if I had it in me for seconds on green bean casserole and stuffing before dessert. That is just so disgusting," Harlow groaned.

"What do you think I was doing when you took Layla up? I snuck seconds so I could be ready for dessert by the time you got out. Now you have to do it just to make me feel better about myself." Lisa wrapped an arm around Harlow and they walked to the stairs together. "How'd she go down?"

"Like a doll. She's beautiful. Perfect and beautiful," Harlow said, thinking it was an understated version of the truth. Layla was even more than that – she was a precious gift. After years of trying without success, Lisa and Steve had been blessed with a miracle.

"I'll call you tonight when she's up at one and four, we'll see if you still feel the same way," Lisa said with an eyebrow raised, but her smile was full of pride and joy.

"Forever and always."

"Yeah, yeah. Do you think you'll stick around for the movie tonight? Mom said she was watching the baby so Steve and I are getting a two-and-a-half-hour night out on the town. For a movie. With the rest of the family," Lisa said, slowly playing out the words to make it seem less exciting as the thought dragged on.

"As appealing as that sounds, I think I'm going to head home. I love the idea of sweatpants and curling up on the couch with a big blanket. And I know your mom already has leftovers packed up for me – the saint – so I'll shamelessly sit surrounded by reheated Tupperware and relish every minute." Harlow grew more excited as she foreshadowed her evening.

"You sure?"

Harlow knew Lisa was asking out of care and concern. Lisa knew going home might be hard, especially on the holiday. But she'd be fine. She might even work up the courage to call her parents or text her brother and sister something more than the usual *Happy Thanksgiving, I love you and miss you.*

"Definitely." Harlow was determined to be independent and find a place in her heart to love the holidays and be thankful for everything she had – not just the pieces of the family she didn't. Besides, she was luckier than most. She had a family. They might have been scattered around the world but she'd take that over any alternative.

"Okay, but if you change your mind, you know where we'll be. Now, let's sneak in and stuff ourselves some more."

—

The snow had left a sparkling dust of white on the sidewalks and streets. It found its way into the creases of signs and stop lights until wintery gusts of wind would come and swoosh it around to land in another nook or cranny.

The beauty of the street lamps had illuminated the ground, causing it to glitter as Harlow drove by. It had drawn her out into the evening for a walk on Grand Avenue after she'd made it home.

It wasn't late, maybe only six or six-thirty, but the sky was dark and she needed those street lamps to light her way.

Tomorrow, the sidewalk would be bustling with Black Friday shoppers loading up with gifts, and lining up outside of the delicious restaurants after working up a hunger from all of their racing around. She loved it here for that very reason.

It hadn't been hard to be the one to stay. To purchase the home that had been given to her and her siblings. It was the perfect house in the perfect neighborhood. Now, looking down the softly lit street that looked like a scene out of a 1940's Christmas movie, it reaffirmed her decision to stay.

But tonight, she'd had the same feeling that had been creeping in over the past couple months, a certain loneliness when she walked through the mansion. *The Hill,* she thought. An immaculate Victorian with endless charm and character.

Growing up it was her haven, her excitement, and her playful escape. That was when she shared it with her family.

The first couple of years after everybody had moved out were nice. She had redecorated, keeping only the furniture and paintings that had the kind of nostalgia that tugged at your heart when you sat on them or looked at it. Everything else – that wasn't of great value and nobody else wanted – was sold in an estate sale, with the profits donated to local charities.

All-in-all, Harlow considered it a win. But after the redecorating and making it her own, the walls seemed too hollow and she found herself longing to have people shuffling around the kitchen, kids running through the halls with their feet stomping and echoing from the floors above, and something other than a blanket keeping her warm at night.

Harlow wrapped her arms tightly around her body at the thought, and the brisk wind swirled around her. As she did, the world around her came back into focus and she noticed a red, round man, opening a box that was nearly the size of himself.

She walked the two short blocks to get closer. She wanted to see what Santa was doing out on Thanksgiving night. Surely Mrs. Claus wanted him home. Surely *he* wanted some of Mrs. Claus' cookies. Harlow chuckled at her thought and shook her head.

"Santa? Hello, can I help you?" Harlow asked, holding back a giggle at the round body tugging at the industrial staples holding the box together – in what seemed to be a steel hold.

"Oh!"

Santa jumped then actually gave a "Ho-Ho-Ho" – the closest thing she'd ever heard to the sound she imagined the real Santa would make.

"Well, didn't you give me a startle." Santa laughed, grabbing his belly. "I would welcome the help if you aren't too cold out here on this beautiful night. It's like the weather knew a little snow would make my day."

It had been a long time since Harlow had believed in Santa Claus, but this man might make her a believer once more. Everything about him was jolly; his voice sounded like a song, and his laugh hit his jiggling belly every time.

"Sure!" Harlow was delighted she could help. "What would you like me to do?"

"I think if you'd be willing to hold the box in place I'd get a good enough grip on it to get it open. It keeps skating in circles every time I try to pull it."

Harlow positioned herself next to Santa and readied herself to push so she could hold the box in position as he pulled.

"One, two-" Santa pulled on three and the staples sounded like tiny fireworks as they popped free from the side of the box. "We did it!"

Santa held his hand high for Harlow to slap it for five as they cheered.

"What's in here?" Harlow asked, trying to peek around the now opened flap.

"Oh, this? This is a miracle maker," Santa said as he rounded the box, removing the rest of the cardboard and foam. "It's a Christmas mailbox."

"For letters to send you?" Harlow could feel herself being drawn into Santa's excitement.

"For that and so much more. Some people, kids and adults alike, have no place to send their Christmas wishes. For things that are more than a gift you can wrap in a box. And sometimes you can't give your wish to a parent, or in some cases there aren't parents to help you send the wish."

Harlow covered her heart with her gloved hand as it broke while she listened and thought about those children who Santa was talking about.

"So, we set up this beautiful Christmas-red mailbox for any and everybody to write and send their Christmas wishes. Some things that are wished for can't be fulfilled, but we sure try our best to come close."

"I love everything about it. It's wonderful." Harlow brushed a small tear away from her blue eyes and pushed a stray curl of red hair behind her ear.

"It really is. Wonderful, that is," Santa agreed and looked at Harlow.

It wasn't the first time he looked at her but this time he stared, pleasantly it seemed, but knowingly, too. Like he saw her through and through.

"You know," he started, "Christmas is for everybody. Sometimes wonderful, magical things can happen by making a simple wish. Perhaps you'll be back. You never know what miracles Christmas can bring."

Harlow smiled at the wise man and his rosy-red cheeks and delicately wiped another tear away.

"Thank you, Santa. I just might."

Harlow leaned in, gave Santa a kiss on his warm cheek, and turned to head home. Thankful she was blessed enough to have one.

KEEP READING

Do you want more of Harlow and Harris?

Click the link, or scan the QR code below to subscribe to Katie's Newsletter and get the bonus epilogue sent straight to your email!

CLICK HERE TO GET YOUR COPY

(Reading a physical copy? Hover your phone over the image!)

BOOKS BY KATIE BACHAND

(click the book title you're interested to navigate to the Amazon sales page!)

SERIES
Becoming Us (Prequel)
Conflict of Interest (#1)
In the Business of Love (#2)
A Business Affair (#3)
Betting on Us (#4)

STANDALONE
The Problem with Love Potions

HOLIDAY
Postmark Christmas
Waiting on Christmas
A Borrowed Christmas Love Story
The Worst Christmas Wife

ABOUT THE AUTHOR

KATIE BACHAND is the author of contemporary romantic comedy and sweet holiday romance.

KATIE lives with her husband, sons, and golden retriever in beautiful Minneapolis, Minnesota. She hopes in her novels, and in life, you find great friendships, great love, and great appreciation for the wonderful world and people in it.

Visit Katie on her website
https://katiebachandauthor.com

Visit Katie on Instagram
https://instagram.com/katiebachandauthor